W9-ATV-049

LESSONS IN LOVE

Lady Marisa Berrington-Crecy had decided to write a book—an amusing, scandalous, gossipy book that would set Edwardian society on its decadent ear. And what better place to gather information than Vox Castle, home of the Duke of Milverley, an attractive widower noted for enjoying the favors of married women.

So Marisa set off disguised as governess to the Duke's young daughter. She was resolved never to fall in love with any man until she met the Duke and found him to be devastatingly handsome. The Duke himself was inflamed by Marisa's pure, innocent beauty—her Titian hair and luminous green eyes.

But one day he unexpectedly discovered her manuscript and, in a violent rage, banished her from his house. Only then did Marisa realize that her one, true love might be lost to her forever.

An intriguing new novel of overwhelming passion by today's best-loved writer of romantic fiction,

BARBARA CARTLAND

Books by BARBARA CARTLAND

Romantic Novels

The Fire of Love
The Unpredictable Bride
Love Holds the Cards
A Virgin in Paris
Love to the Rescue
Love Is Contraband
The Enchanting Evil
The Unknown Heart
The Secret Fear
The Reluctant Bride

The Pretty Horse-Breakers
The Audacious Adventuress
Lost Enchantment
Halo for the Devil
The Irresistible Buck
The Complacent Wife
The Odious Duke
The Daring Deception
No Darkness for Love
The Little Adventure

Lessons in Love

Autobiographical and Biographical

The Isthmus Years 1919–1939
The Years of Opportunity 1939–1945
I Search for Rainbows 1945–1966
We Danced All Night 1919–1929
Ronald Cartland
 (with a Foreword by Sir Winston Churchill)
Polly, my Wonderful Mother

Historical

Bewitching Women
The Outrageous Queen
 (The Story of Queen Christina of Sweden)
The Scandalous Life of King Carol
The Private Life of King Charles II
The Private Life of Elizabeth, Empress of Austria
Josephine, Empress of France
Diane de Poitiers
Metternich—the Passionate Diplomat

Sociology

You in the Home
The Fascinating Forties
Marriage for Moderns
Be Vivid, Be Vital
Love, Life and Sex
Look Lovely, Be Lovely
Vitamins for Vitality
Husbands and Wives

Etiquette
The Many Facets of Love
Sex and the Teenager
The Book of Charm
Living Together
Woman—The Enigma
The Youth Secret
The Magic of Honey

Barbara Cartland's Health Food Cookery Book
Barbara Cartland's Book of Beauty and Health
Barbara Cartland's Book of Useless Information

Lessons In Love

BARBARA CARTLAND

LESSONS IN LOVE
A Bantam Book / published March 1974
2nd printing
3rd printing

All rights reserved.
Copyright © 1974 by Barbara Cartland.
This book may not be reproduced in whole or in part, by
mimeograph or any other means, without permission.
For information address: Bantam Books, Inc.

Bantam Books are published by Bantam Books, Inc. Its trade-
mark, consisting of the words "Bantam Books" and the por-
trayal of a bantam, is registered in the United States Patent
Office and in other countries. Marca Registrada. Bantam
Books, Inc., 666 Fifth Avenue, New York, New York 10019.

PRINTED IN THE UNITED STATES OF AMERICA

Author's Note

While the hero and heroine of this book are fictitious the descriptions of the Marlborough House Set in 1890 are authentic. Lady Brooke captivated the heart of Prince of Wales for ten years. In 1893 "Brookee" became the Earl of Warwick, but the previous year the fascinating Daisy had been converted to Socialism.

Unlike her contemporaries she really cared about the poor, the aged, the miners and the workers. Despite the success of conventional society, she spent the whole of her huge private fortune on philanthropic schemes.

At this time the Prince of Wales was extremely superstitious and would never sit down thirteen for a meal and the mattresses were never turned on a Friday if he was staying in a private home.

Mr. Arthur Balfour became Prime Minister when Edward became King. He died the first Earl of Balfour and a bachelor. His love affair with the Viscountess Elcho was in the great Edwardian tradition and lasted from the year of her marriage, 1883, until his death in 1922.

Chapter One
1890

"I do not want to be unkind," the new Countess of Berrington said, "but I do feel that as I am only thirty-five it would be quite incongruous for me to chaperon a young girl."

She looked at her niece by marriage almost defiantly as she spoke; they both knew that Lady Berrington would be forty next birthday.

"Do not upset yourself, Aunt Kitty," Marisa replied. "I have no intention of being launched into the social world. I have done it once and I assure you it was the most unpleasant experience of my life."

"Nonsense!" Lady Berrington said, "you must have enjoyed your Season in London."

"I hated every moment of it!" Marisa answered almost passionately. "Cousin Octavia certainly did her best. She took me to Ball after Ball, to Hurlingham, to Henley and Ranelagh. I was in the Royal enclosure at Ascot and I was presented to the Queen at Buckingham Palace."

She paused and her eyes twinkled.

"Her Majesty looked at me down her nose, and my curtsey was so awkward that I very nearly sprawled at her feet."

"You were only seventeen then," Lady Berrington said. "You would enjoy London now. The only difficulty is whom we can persuade to chaperone you?"

"I have already said," Marisa replied, "that I have no intention of coming to London. But I do need your help, Aunt Kitty."

"My help?" Lady Berrington exclaimed and raised her eye-brows.

It was, as she was well aware, one of her most attractive mannerisms and was continually admired by the dashing young men who frequented her house and who apparently were tolerated without comment by her good-natured husband.

"I need your help, Aunt Kitty," Marisa explained, "because I intend to become a governess."

"A governess?"

The Countess of Berrington could not have been more astonished if a bomb had exploded in the room.

"But why? For what reason?"

To her surprise her niece looked over her shoulder as if to be quite certain that no-one was listening.

"If I let you into a secret, Aunt Kitty," she said, "will you swear not to reveal it to Uncle George or to anyone else?"

"Yes, of course," Lady Berrington replied, "but I cannot imagine what on earth your secret could be."

"I am writing a book," Marisa said.

"A book?" Again the pretty, dark eye-brows arched upwards. "Do you mean a novel?"

"I mean nothing of the sort," Marisa replied positively. "I am in fact writing about the Scandals of Society."

"Marisa, you must be joking!" Lady Berrington cried. "And it is n_. `- particularly good taste."

"No, I am serious," Marisa answered. "Mr. Charles Bradlough, before he became a Member of Parliament, prepared a pamphlet entitled 'Impeachment of the House of Brunswick'. Papa was very amused by it, but I thought it was too pompously written to have any real impact."

"What on earth do you mean by that?" Lady Berrington asked.

"I mean," Marisa replied, "that I intend to write an amusing, scandalous, gossipy book that everyone will read and which will show up Society in its true colours."

"And what may that be?" Lady Berrington enquired in bewilderment.

"In my opinion," Marisa answered, "it is a hot-bed of immorality, extravagance and irresponsibility."

The Countess put back her head and laughed, but at the same time she looked uneasy.

"You must be playing a joke on me, Marisa. I cannot

conceive for one moment that you would really do anything so outrageous, so calculated to upset Uncle George and myself, as even to talk in such a manner, let alone write it down."

"I am deadly serious," Marisa said. "But I promise you, Aunt Kitty, that you and Uncle George will be quite safe. I will naturally not sign the book with my own name."

"That is a relief at any rate," the Countess said, "but at the same time the whole idea is completely ridiculous. What do you know about Society?"

"If you are interested I will tell you," Marisa answered. "When I was going through the family papers, I discovered the diaries of Great-Aunt Augusta."

"Who was she?" Lady Berrington asked wrinkling her smooth white brow.

"She lived a hundred years ago when the Prince of Wales, later George IV, was causing scandal after scandal, when it was considered smart to be eccentric and the extravagance of the Bucks and Rakes frequenting Carlton House was an appalling contrast to the abject poverty and misery to be seen everywhere in the streets of London."

"What had your Great-Aunt Augusta got to do with it?" the Countess asked in a bewildered tone.

"She wrote a very amusing and graphic diary of what was going on in social circles," Marisa answered. "I intend to use her diary to reveal the behaviour not only of Royal personages, but of Society toadying them up to the present day."

"You certainly know nothing of what is going on now," Kitty Berrington said sharply.

"You would be surprised at what one learns just from the pages of the *Times*," Marisa answered. "Look at what was happening in the 60's. What about the nephew and heir of the Earl of Wicklow who died in a brothel and whose wife tried to pass off an adopted child as his next of kin? And Papa knew Lord Willoughby d'Eresby, Joint Hereditary Grand Chamberlain of England, who fleeced his French mistress of thousands of pounds and then ran off with her maid!"

"I do not believe it!" the Countess said in a strangled tone.

"I assure you it is true," Marisa answered, "and Lord Euston, son and heir of Duke Grafton, made a disastrous marriage with a very vulgar woman and thought he was free when he discovered she was a bigamist, only to learn later that he was legally married, because her first husband had also been a bigamist."

"I cannot think where you get hold of such stories!" Lady Berrington cried. "And anyway that is all in the past."

"Is it?" Marisa asked. "What about the Prince of Wales' infatuation for Mrs. Lily Langtry? The letters he wrote to Lady Aylesford which Lord Randolph Churchill threatened to publish and the Tranby Croft scandal this year when his Royal Highness had to appear in the witness-box? You must have read what the papers said about the Prince's gambling baccarat-playing friends!"

"Will you be quiet . . ." Lady Berrington began.

"And no-one knows better than you, Aunt Kitty," Marisa continued relentlessly, "that everyone is now gossiping about H.R.H.'s passion for the fascinating Lady Brooke."

"I will not listen to any more!" Lady Berrington shouted in a furious tone. "Do you realise, Marisa, that if one word of this conversation was even whispered at Marlborough House, George and I would be completely ruined?"

Her voice dropped as she continued:

"We would not be asked to any of the houses we visit now, and the Prince would refuse to have us included in any dinner party where he was present! What is more you would doubtless be had up for libel, and we should see our names emblazoned all over the vulgar newspapers!"

"I promise you, Aunt Kitty, my book will be far too clever for that," Marisa answered. "There will be dashes and dots instead of full names, but everybody will know to whom I am referring. It is very unlikely that anyone will come forward to challenge the assertions I make, when a great number of them have already been aired in public."

"You are crazy!" Lady Berrington cried. "I wash my hands of you! It is all your father's fault. George has said often enough that if his brother had not been an Earl he would have been a revolutionary or an anarchist."

Marisa laughed, a soft musical laugh of pure amusement.

"We call ourselves Radicals. But dear Papa was very revolutionary and he hated Society."

"For a very good reason," Lady Berrington said with a spiteful note in her voice.

"If you are referring to my Mama," Marisa answered, "of course Papa was jealous and upset when she ran away with Lord Geltsdale. But after all, as he refused to divorce her it was not the sort of scandal that you fear, it was not headlined in the press."

"But everyone knew," Lady Berrington said, "of course they knew! George said he was humiliated even in his Clubs at the things that were said! Your mother caused a terrible family scandal, Marisa, and it seems as if you are going to try to do the same thing."

"Well, I can promise you one thing," Marisa replied, "I am going to run away with no-one and as I do not intend ever to get married, you need not fear that I shall disgrace you by turning up in the Divorce Court."

"What do you mean you do not intend to get married?" Lady Berrington asked crossly. "It is the best thing that could happen to you! Get married, Marisa, to the first man who asks you, and stop all this nonsense about writing books which will destroy us all."

"You mean it might destroy your social life," Marisa said coolly. "Well, as long as you will help me, Aunt Kitty, I promise you I will take the greatest care not to do anything which might in any way implicate you or Uncle George."

"What do you want me to do?" Lady Berrington asked apprehensively.

"I want you to get me a situation as a governess in some really important household. I want to see for myself how its owners behave. I want to be quite certain that the stories I have been told are true and that Papa was not exaggerating. You know how violently antagonistic he was towards the nobility, typified of course by Lord Geltsdale."

"Your father was a fanatic on the subject," Lady Berrington said angrily.

"Papa used to say," Marisa reminisced, "that Guy

Fawkes made a great mistake. He should not have tried to blow up the House of Commons, but to demolish the House of Lords."

"Please, Marisa, give up this ridiculous idea," the Countess pleaded, making what was obviously a great effort to be conciliatory. "Throw away Great-Aunt Augusta's diaries and lead a normal life, like any other girl of your age. After all you are only twenty-one and we all have crazy ideas when we are young."

"But I enjoy writing!" Marisa replied. "I am sorry, Aunt Kitty, if it upsets you. Perhaps it would have been better not to tell you, but I really do need your assistance if I am to get a post in an important house which will be of help to me."

"Help to you!" Lady Berrington exclaimed in a strangled voice. "You make me feel faint with apprehension and horror. As to getting you into a house of one of my friends, do you not think they will realise who is writing about them?"

"Why should they?" Marisa enquired. "I am not so half-witted as to take a post of governess in my own name. I have already decided that I will call myself Mitton."

"Why Mitton?" Lady Berrington enquired.

"I think Marisa Mitton sounds so prim, subdued and governess-like," Marisa explained. "After all, one could hardly expect anyone to employ someone called Lady Marisa Berrington-Crecy. They would find it an embarrassment."

"They would find it an embarrassment to employ you in any circumstances," Lady Berrington said spitefully.

She rose from her chair as she spoke and walked across her sitting-room with its elegant little tables of knick-knacks and bric-à-brac, with its draped piano covered in silver-framed photographs, and the silk damask curtains fringed and caught back with huge silk tassels.

She looked very pretty in her dress of black silk with bands of crepe edging the full skirt. Her fair hair was fashionably arranged in the fashion set by Princess Alexandra under a small bonnet from which flowed a heavy black veil.

The Countess had just come in from driving when her

niece was announced and now agitatedly she drew her
long black kid-gloves from her hands and twisted them together feverishly as she said:

"I just cannot believe what you have been saying to me,
Marisa. What you ask is impossible, absolutely impossible! Besides, my dear girl, who would employ you as a
governess? Have you not looked at yourself in a mirror?"

She turned round as she spoke to stare at her niece, to
see the Venetian red hair with touches of gold in it which
framed a small pointed face with an incredibly white skin.

She noted also with no satisfaction that Marisa's large
green eyes were fringed with long, naturally dark eyelashes and that her mouth owing nothing to artifice was
provocatively red.

"You look exactly like your mother," she said disparag-
ingly. "Of course I was only a child when I saw her, but
she had hair like yours and a face which, I assure you,
would have discouraged any lady in her senses from en-
gaging her as a governess."

"But I have to be a governess!" Marisa asserted. "Do
you not understand, Aunt Kitty, there are only two
careers open to a lady! A governess or a companion. If I
become a companion, I shall be shut up with some old
woman in the wilds of the country! I shall learn nothing
there."

She paused and then, with a sideways glance under
her eyelashes that was extremely mischievous, she said:

"Of course the alternative would be for you to
chaperone me for at least one Season. I could then meet
all your smart friends!"

She could see the expression of horror on her aunt's
face as she added:

"I am sure Uncle George would understand. After all
you and he will soon, I imagine, be moving into Berrington Park, so I shall have no home."

"I will not chaperone you! I will not, whatever George
may say," Lady Berrington said angrily. "I am much too
young, Marisa, to be a chaperone and to have to sit on a
dais with the Dowagers. And besides you are too pretty,
you know that!"

"I am glad I look like my mother," Marisa said. "Apparently everyone thought she was very beautiful, al-

though Mrs. Featherstone-Haugh, when she came to stay, used to tell me that Mama was a *femme fatale* from the moment she left the school-room."

"Mrs. Featherstone-Haugh!" Lady Berrington exclaimed in a tone of disgust. "If there ever was a spiteful old gossip; it was that woman. She always hated me and she always made mischief. If that is where you have been getting your information about Society, I can assure you, Marisa, it will be poisonously exaggerated."

"Mrs. Featherstone-Haugh was certainly amusing," Marisa smiled. "She used to save up all the most scandalous tit-bits to tell Papa, and of course I listened. I think she was the only woman besides Mama that he was ever interested in, but she knew her hold over him depended largely on her service as a source of information."

"You must realise, Marisa, that your father's loathing of Society, which stemmed entirely from the way your mother treated him, was abnormal," Lady Berrington said. "But you are supposed to be intelligent. So now your father is dead you can forget that fanatical hatred with which he viewed the world for so many years."

"Mama ran away when I was only five," Marisa said, "so I had quite a lot of time to be imbued with Papa's ideas. After all, Aunt Kitty, no-one has worried about me very much until now."

"I always thought you were happy at the Park," Lady Perrington said uneasily.

"It suited you to think so," Marisa said quietly and without any resentment in her voice.

"Please, Marisa, give up this ridiculous idea," the Countess begged. "I will get your uncle to give you an allowance. After all, if your father had not died, no doubt there would have been enough money for you to be at least comfortable."

She drew in her breath.

"But though we are desperately hard up for all the things we want to do, George will not only give you enough pin-money to have decent clothes, but I will find you someone really nice with whom you can live. I am sure, your Cousin Alice would be delighted to have you."

Marisa laughed.

"If you imagine, Aunt Kitty, that I would go to that

mausoleum in Brighton and spend the rest of my life taking Cousin Alice's pug for a walk, you are very much mistaken! No, I have decided what I am going to do, and if you want me to be very discreet and not in any way upset the smart and exclusive circle in which you move, then you must help me."

"This is blackmail, Marisa, that is what it is!"

"Something in which most people indulge when they want their own way," Marisa replied.

"I tell you it is impossible," Lady Berrington said. "Can you imagine what the Duchess of Richmond, the Duchess of Portland or Lady Brooke would think of inviting someone who looks like you to look after their children? You are too young for one thing."

"I shall say I am twenty-five," Marisa answered, "and if I drag back my hair I can look quite prim."

She paused a moment, then added:

"Of course I could dye it."

"Do not be so absurd!" Lady Berrington exclaimed. "Dyed hair always looks dyed, and that would make you appear even more peculiar than you do at the moment. It is all very well to bully me, Marisa, but I have told you there is nobody, no . . ."

She stopped suddenly.

"I have an idea," she said, "but, no . . . it is impossible!"

"Why is it impossible?" Marisa asked.

"Because you are not suitable to be a governess to any child, not even to Valerius' daughter, who I believe is half mad."

"Valerius!" Marisa replied in a strange voice. "Do you mean the Duke of Milverley?"

"Yes, of course," Lady Berrington said. "We were staying at Vox Castle two weeks ago, and somebody was telling me, I have forgotten who it was, that the child is quite out of control. She is only nine or ten and has already had dozens of governesses. Not one of them will stay."

"What has happened to the Duchess?" Marisa asked.

"She is dead," the Countess replied. "A strange neurotic creature, she died when the child was born. There was

never a chance of Valerius and her being suited to each
other."

"Then why did they get married?" Marisa asked.

"Oh it is a long story," the Countess answered. "The
Duke was in love, when he grew up, with the beautiful
and imperious Countess de Grey. He obviously could not
marry her and the story is that she was quite unnecessarily
unkind to him, being at the time in love with a much
older man."

"Naturally not her husband," Marisa said sarcastically.

"Of course not!" Lady Berrington agreed and continued. "Then I have always understood that on the rebound
the Duke was tricked into proposing to the Marquis of
Dorset's daughter, a hysterical creature, who I believe disliked him as much as he disliked her."

She lowered her voice.

"Everyone heard tales of their rows and quarrels. She
used to get up in the middle of a dinner-party and flounce
out because she was annoyed at something he had said.
Anyway when she died it was a great relief to everyone,
but apparently the child is just like her."

"As you have stayed at Vox have you not seen the
girl?" Marisa asked.

"Valerius has never mentioned her in my presence," the
Countess replied, "and I assure you, Marisa, I have something better to do than wander round other people's nurseries. I have quite enough trouble with my own!"

"What about recommending me to the Duke as a suitable governess for his daughter?"

"I naturally should not write to him," Lady Berrington
snapped. "All the arrangements in the house are made by
a Miss Whitcham, who is the Duke's secretary and has
been at Vox since time immemorial. She was employed by
his mother for years."

"Then do write to her," Marisa urged. "After all, you
have nothing to lose. If they have so much trouble with
governesses, they might like to have someone sensible for
a change."

"Sensible!" Lady Berrington exclaimed. "If you think
you are sensible, Marisa, you must be blind, deaf and
dumb! But at least if I get you accepted you will realise

what a deadly life it is, trudging round with somebody else's tiresome child."

"You really will write and recommend me?" Marisa asked.

"I will write, and a great deal of good it will do you!" Lady Berrington replied sharply.

"Then do it now," Marisa prompted, "I do not trust you not to change your mind after I have gone."

"Really, Marisa, you are the most exasperating girl I have ever met in the whole of my life," Lady Berrington said. "All I can say is that I hope this book you are writing shows a little more patience and understanding."

The Countess paused and looked at her niece speculatively.

"Why are you so vitriolic against the social world?" she asked. "I can understand your father's attitude. After all no man likes to be made to look a fool because his wife finds another man more attractive than himself. But you have never had an opportunity to get your heart broken; so what has jaundiced your outlook on life?"

"I do not think you would understand if I told you," Marisa said evasively. "Write the letter, Aunt Kitty, and then I will disappear. You do not want Uncle George to find me here and ask too many questions about what I am going to do with myself."

She smiled.

"I suggest you tell him that I have gone to stay with friends in the North of England, if he takes the trouble to enquire, which I doubt he will."

"Your Uncle George has always been very fond of you," Lady Berrington said with a singular lack of conviction in her voice.

She sat down at the writing-table.

"What shall I say are your qualifications?" she enquired. "I presume you have some?"

"I speak French and Italian," Marisa replied. "I can read Latin and play the piano."

"I cannot believe that a child of nine will need more than that. I have always said it is a mistake to educate girls," Lady Berrington snapped. "I can assure you that mine shall know as little as possible. If there is one thing a man avoids at all costs, it is a clever woman."

"As I wish to be avoided, that just suits me," Marisa said.

Her Aunt glanced at her as she stood at the window, the sunshine glinting on her glorious red hair under an unfashionable black bonnet. Her skin was very white and her eyes seemed enormous in her pale face. But her dress was of cheap serge and extremely badly made.

It was perhaps a twinge of conscience which made Lady Berrington say:

"You will want some clothes if you are going to Vox. Although you will be only the governess you might have to escort the child downstairs. Anyway I advise you not to wear black."

"I thought that it seemed rather appropriate," Marisa said, "although Papa always said mourning was a heathenish tradition which should be abandoned."

"With your hair and skin, black is far too sensational," Lady Berrington said. "I shall have to wear it of course for at least nine months—George will insist. But it could not be more annoying, because I have just bought quite a number of attractive gowns which will be completely out of fashion by the time I can wear them. I had better give them to you, Marisa. We are about the same size."

Marisa's face lit up in a smile.

"Do you mean that, Aunt Kitty? I should be extremely grateful! Apart from having no money to spend on clothes, I do loathe standing for hours and having pins stuck into me while I am fitted."

"The trouble about you, Marisa," her Aunt said, "is that you have no feminine attributes. Women should like clothes, they should want to go to Balls, they should long to be married, and they should not want to write books."

"Can a leopard change his spots?" Marisa laughed. "I am set in my ways, Aunt Kitty, and if they are ways into which Papa has led me, the relations have no-one to blame but themselves. Do you know that when Papa died last month, it was over two years since any of his relations had communicated with him?"

"And whose fault was that?" Lady Berrington enquired. "When we did write to your father, we either got no answer at all or he replied in a rude manner."

"All the same," Marisa said, her voice softening, "I

think he was often lonely. He wanted to see his brother and he wanted to feel he was of importance to somebody besides me."

"Well it is too late now," Lady Berrington said lightly. "Here is the letter, Marisa, and God help us all if you let me down."

"I will not, I promise you," Marisa said. "Incidentally I think I shall be a rather good governess. I might even be able to stuff some knowledge into the head of the wretched child whom nobody seems to want."

"I did not say that!" Lady Berrington cried. "I merely said that the Duke has never mentioned her to me. For all I know he may dote on his daughter. He is always with the Prince, and his Royal Highness is devoted to children. As you know, Emily is his god-daughter."

Lady Berrington picked up a photograph from the piano as she spoke and held it towards Marisa.

"This is a picture of Emily," she said. "You see how pretty she is growing."

Marisa looked at the stereotyped stiff photograph of a little girl staring into the camera obviously dressed in her best.

She wondered if she imagined a resemblance in those slightly protruding eyes and rather full mouth to the Heir to the Throne.

She was well aware that five years ago her father had said some very scathing things about the attention the Prince of Wales was paying to his attractive sister-in-law.

It was extraordinary how Papa, living quietly in Berrington Park, had always seemed to know what was going on in the gay circle which surrounded the Prince and his lovely Danish wife.

But there was no restriction on gossip and even in the country they learned of the Prince's infatuation for this beauty or that, and the manner in which the Queen, encarcerated at Windsor, was shocked and disgusted by the behaviour of what was called "the Marlbrough House Set".

Lady Berrington sealed the letter, stamped it and handed it to Marisa.

"Post it yourself," she said, "and then you will know that I have kept my word."

Marisa looked down at the large white envelope addressed to Miss Whitcham, c/o His Grace the Duke of Milverley, Vox Castle, Kent.

"Will you let me know when you get a reply?" she asked.

"Are you going back to Berrington?" the Countess enquired.

"I have no wish to stay in London," Marisa answered. "I will wait until I hear from you and then I can come and collect the clothes you have promised me."

Her Aunt sat looking at her reflectively.

"You know, Marisa," she said, "if you took trouble with yourself you could be a great success. I am not being unkind in refusing to chaperon you, it is really a instinct for self-preservation. You are far too pretty! And even though you have no dowry, I am sure it would be easy to find you a wealthy, perhaps important husband."

She paused.

"Give up the ridiculous idea of writing a book," she went on, "and I will find someone who has a daughter of your age who would be prepared to chaperon you for a small fee."

Marisa's face lit up in a smile.

"You are being very kind, Aunt Kitty," she said, "and I do appreciate it, but the answer is no. I know exactly what I want to do, I have it all planned out. I cannot think of any house I would rather visit than Vox."

"Why?" Lady Berrington enquired.

"That is something I might tell you one day," Marisa said, "but not until after I have been accepted for the position of governess there."

It was five days later that Marisa, writing in the study that her father had always used at Berrington Park, received a telegram.

"You are to proceed to Vox immediately. Pick up baggage when passing through London."
                                              Kitty Berrington

Marisa read it through twice and then she gave a little exclamation of sheer joy. She had won!

It was not a victory of which she had been completely

confident. But she had succeeded in persuading or rather threatening her aunt into doing what she wished, and now she was to go to Vox Castle.

She walked across the room to stand looking out at the badly kept lawn which had been neglected through lack of gardeners ever since Marisa could remember.

Her father, interested only in his papers and books, and in his vendetta against the ruling classes, had been a hopeless organiser where the Estate was concerned. He never remembered either to collect the rents from his tenants himself, or to appoint anyone to collect them for him.

His farms were neglected, he was robbed right and left by those he did employ, and the house was falling into disrepair.

Marisa was well aware that the new Earl, her father's younger brother, was going to find it a difficult task and a very expensive one to get things straight again.

It was one of the reasons why she had no wish to add to her Uncle's liabilities—apart from the fact that she was determined to carry on the battle in which her father had been engaged all the years while she had been growing up.

She had been fired by his enthusiasm, exhilarated by his contempt for the weaklings, spendthrifts and wasters who called themselves nobility.

Her father's Radical views and his revolutionary suggestions for sweeping reforms seemed to her extremely practical, besides the fact that like himself she had a personal vendetta against Society.

It had been with a belated sense of responsibility towards his daughter that the Earl of Berrington had sent her to London when she was only seventeen to make her début under the chaperonage of a cousin whom he had not seen for some years.

Badly dressed, completely unversed in the social graces, Marisa had suffered agonies of shyness and embarrassment.

She had committed gaffe after gaffe mostly through ignorance. She had smarted under snubs and felt humiliated by the laughter of those who found her countrified manners amusing and her clothes a joke.

She had found that she had nothing to say to the young

men who were forced by her cousin into asking her to
dance, or who had sat bored and indifferent on either side
of her at dinner-parties.

She had not understood then what was wrong.

She had only known that she was acutely miserable and
that she longed with a homesickness which became almost
a physical pain for her free life at Berrington Park, for her
horses, her dogs and her father's interesting and enlivening
discourses.

It was Mrs. Featherstone-Haugh who finally forced her
to realise that being able to converse is an essential of
good manners and that a guest must pay for hospitality by
being pleasant, charming and amenable.

She also learnt that it was a woman's job to look attractive and to grace a room as if she were a bowl of flowers.

. As she grew more mature, as she became aware of her
own beauty, Marisa became more assured and self-confi-
dent, but those hideous months in London when she was
seventeen remained like a scar upon her memory.

They had all culminated, she thought now, with something that had happened at the Ball which had been given
by Cousin Alice.

Marisa could remember the misery of receiving the
guests, standing with her hostess beside Florence who
shared the honours of the ball with her.

It was by no means only a débutante dance, because
Cousin Alice being a Marchioness had the entrée to all
the most exclusive houses in London and was determined
to entertain her own friends at the same time that she
launched her daughter.

There was the usual array of Devonshires, Richmonds,
Portlands and Beauforts with or without their children.

All were glittering with a profusion of tiaras and decorations in honour not, alas, of the Prince of Wales, but of
one of Queen Victoria's less glamorous children—Princess
Beatrice.

Marisa, after having been taken down to supper by a
chinless youth who could talk only of racing, and finding
herself without a partner, went in search of Cousin Alice
so that she could stand conventionally by her side.

She could not find her, and wandering through the Reception-Rooms she came from behind a pillar to see two people seated on a sofa with their backs to her.

She was just about to creep past when she heard a lady resplendent in emeralds say:

"Do be careful, Valerius, you know how people gossip!"

"Do you think that worries me?" the gentleman asked in a deep voice which somehow arrested Marisa's attention. "You are very alluring, Dolly, as you well know."

"I should make you do your duty," the lady replied with a light laugh. "Instead of talking to me for what has been far too long, you should go and dance with the girls for whom this party is given. Remember, Valerius, you are a very eligible *parti*."

"Do you really think I would waste my attractions on that moon-faced creature with vacant eyes," the gentleman replied mockingly, "or the red-headed one who looks as if she were a carrot that had been pulled too soon?"

Marisa had crept away, she felt somehow it was the final blow in a long series of insults to be described in such a manner.

Despite all her cousin's protestations, she had returned home the following day, making an excuse that her father was ill and needed her presence.

It had not been difficult to learn who the man was who had spoken of her in such a manner. There was only one important member of Society with the unusual Christian name of Valerius.

The Duke of Milverley was frequently mentioned in the papers, his magnificent house, Vox Castle, described, sketched and photographed. Marisa grew used to seeing the Duke's features.

She had not seen him in the flesh, she had only heard his voice, but she felt she would have recognised anywhere the high imperious nose, the firm almost cruel mouth, the square chin and above all the cynical expression in his eyes and the deep lines running from nose to mouth.

"I hate him," Marisa had thought that evening as she left the Ball-room to find sanctuary in the Ladies' Cloakroom on the second floor.

"I hate him," she said aloud as she drove back to Berrington.

It was as if her hatred of the Duke drove her into identifying herself still more fully with her father's contempt for the ruling classes.

When the Earl paid his infrequent visits to the House of Lords, Marisa would ply him with questions about whom he had seen and what had been discussed.

And yet, for some reason she could not explain to herself, she could never bring herself to ask specifically if the Duke of Milverley had been present.

She had hoped her father would mention his name, but he never did, and finally she came to the conclusion that like so many of his contemporaries the Duke did not care about his country, the political and social implications of the Bills that were passed, or the reforms that were an urgent necessity.

"The absentee Peers are all despicable," she told herself, "and the Duke who is so wealthy and so influential, is the worst of them all."

Yet now she was going to Vox and she would be under the same roof as the Duke.

She had a strange feeling that fate was bringing her together with the man she most disliked, the man who had disparaged her, the man who had driven her hot-foot from London, and who had confirmed and accentuated her hatred of men.

Marisa pulled open a drawer in the desk at which she habitually sat. It had pleased her father that she should write in the same room as himself.

At first he had made her copy out his articles, his endless letters to *The Times* and the memoranda which he sent by the hundred to his fellow Peers and Members of the Commons.

Then he had encouraged her to write, not under her own name, but using a "nom de plume," with which Editors became increasingly familiar.

She had had letters published in *The Morning Post*, the *Review of Reviews*, *The Fortnightly* and this year, a great triumph, in the new Labour Journal, *The Clarion*!

Her father's desk was piled with papers which Marisa

had not yet sorted out since his death, but her own was neat and tidy. She disliked working in a muddle.

She pulled open one of the drawers, put her hand to the back of it and pulled out two letters.

She sat looking at them. The envelopes were written in a hurried rather untidy hand, they were worn and creased, and the writing was smudged as if they had been handled many times.

Marisa stared at them for a moment with a strange expression on her face.

Then very slowly, without drawing the letters from the envelopes, she tore them up. Smaller and smaller she made the pieces until they were nothing but fragments.

Then she threw them into the waste-paper basket.

This was the end, the end of something she had treasured, a tenderness that she had been unable to forget for a man who had thought her merely an attractive neighbour and to whom she had meant nothing—absolutely nothing.

Just for a moment Marisa could not help a pang of regret that she had torn up the only mementos that she had of him.

He had come to see her father about a foal he wished to buy.

He had been tall and handsome, and to a girl starved of male companionship he had seemed, as he walked into the dingy and dilapidated hall, almost like a Greek God.

"How do you do," he said, "I am Harry Huntingdon. I have been told that Lord Berrington has a foal for sale. I am building up a stud on an Estate I have just bought about ten miles away from here."

"Will you come in to the study, Mr. Huntingdon?" Marisa had asked shyly.

"Actually," he smiled. "I am Sir Harold Huntingdon, if we have to be formal."

"I am sorry," she said hastily.

"Do not be," he said, "I am delighted for you to call me whatever comes to your mind. If the foal is as good-looking as you, then I shall want to buy it, whatever the price."

She looked up at him and felt as if her heart stopped beating.

"Come and show me the animal before I see your father," Harry Huntingdon suggested and of course she agreed.

It had been the prelude for quite a number of visits. It appeared that he wanted to see the foal, the dam, the sire, and only Marisa could show them to him.

He paid her compliments, he flirted with her with the expertise of a man who manages to make every woman he speaks to think that she is the most important woman in his life.

At the end of a week Marisa thought herself in love with him. He asked her to meet him in the early morning and they went riding over the country-side.

She did not realise that he treated her as a pretty child who amused him and that he was too much of a gentleman to take advantage of her quite obvious infatuation.

It was only after three weeks of ecstasy that she learnt he was married and that his wife, who had been away from home on a visit, was returning the following day.

When Harry Huntingdon told her that they could not continue to go riding together because his wife would be jealous, she felt as if she had been struck by a bullet in the breast.

She had gone home blindly and felt violently sick for three days, after which she had resolutely put him out of her mind.

But she could never bring herself to destroy the only two letters she had from him, just little notes asking her to meet him at some particular place on the Estate. They were all she had left!

Now she thought it was almost laughable that he should have changed her whole attitude towards men.

But she knew if she was honest that it was not only her feelings towards Harry which were responsible for her decision never to marry, but because she was determined that never would she run the risk of behaving as her mother had and running away to leave behind a forgotten and unwanted child.

She could remember crying at night because she was lonely, because there was no-one to kiss her before she went to bed, because her whole body ached for someone warm and soft and loving on whom she could depend.

It had not made her hate the mother who had deserted her, but rather she loathed with a violent physical emotion the man who had tempted her away.

"He was so dashing, so attractive, a man no woman could resist!"

How often had she heard Lord Geltsdale described in such terms when no-one had thought she was listening.

"You know, Lionel," she had heard Mrs. Featherstone-Haugh once say to her father, "you cannot really blame Clarice. Lord Geltsdale was a lady-killer if ever there was one! She never really had a chance once he set his eyes on her."

Marisa had not waited to hear her father's reply, she had merely gone from the room hating men who were "lady-killers," who tempted women away from their husbands and who raised false hopes in the hearts of foolish little girls.

Men! They were the enemy, they were the hazard she must avoid for the rest of her life!

Marisa rose and walked again towards the window. Tomorrow she was going to Vox. She had striven so violently to get her own way, but now she felt a strange reluctance to embark upon the unknown.

Then a picture of the Duke's cynical face came to her mind.

"I will show him up," she told herself, "I will put him in my book, I will portray him so vividly that people shall see him for what he is! I will make him a laughing-stock! I will make even those who toady to him feel disgusted and repelled by him."

She gave a little laugh! This would be her revenge, the book which would set the social world by the ears!

The very thought of her future success made her feel strong and no longer afraid.

Chapter Two

Travelling toward Vox Castle, Marisa thought with sheer delight of what lay ahead.

She had decided to be extravagant and to travel first class so the compartment was comfortable and uncrowded. The train was due to arrive early in the afternoon.

She had reached her aunt's house in London at breakfast time and had been kept waiting for nearly an hour before the Countess would see her.

Finally she went upstairs to the ornate and luxurious bed-room, to find Lady Berrington sitting in front of her mirror while a maid arranged her hair.

"That will do, Rose," she said as her niece appeared, "I want to talk to Lady Marisa alone."

The maid withdrew and the Countess turned round on her dressing-table stool to face Marisa.

"Is there any chance you have changed your mind?" she asked.

"No of course not, Aunt Kitty," Marisa replied. "Good morning, and thank you for sending me the telegram."

"They have obviously lost yet another governess at Vox," Lady Berrington said. "But, Marisa, I have not been able to sleep at nights, thinking of this terrible book you are writing and what ghastly harm it might do to us all."

"I have promised you that I will not in any way incriminate either you or Uncle George," Marisa answered. "No-one shall ever know who the writer is."

"Give it up! I beg of you, give it up!" Lady Berrington said with real feeling in her voice. "I am afraid, desperately afraid, Marisa, that someone will discover the identity of the author and then we will never be forgiven. Never! Never!"

"I promise you that will not happen, Aunt Kitty," Marisa said soothingly, "and now tell me what you have heard from Vox."

"I merely had a telegram in answer to my letter," Lady Berrington said. "It was of course from Miss Whitcham and she said that I was to send you at once. I had the telegram somewhere but it seems to have vanished."

She looked vaguely about the room.

"And did you reply?" Marisa enquired.

"Yes, I sent her a wire last night to say you would be leaving today. You have enough money for the fare I suppose? It will be naturally refunded to you."

"I have plenty of money," Marisa replied. "I am so grateful, really grateful, Aunt Kitty. I promise you I will try not to bother you again, since you have done me the one good turn that I asked you for."

"If you really wish to do me a good turn, you would not go," Lady Berrington said. "I am so nervous, Marisa, that I believe I would almost rather chaperon you than let you write this crazy book."

"Even if you chaperon me, I would still write it," Marisa said.

"You are hopeless!" Lady Berrington exclaimed sharply.

She turned round towards the mirror, staring at her reflection as if the very pretty picture she presented gave her some comfort.

"The clothes are upstairs," she said. "Rose has packed everything. It is really quite a trousseau. How nice it would be if you were going to be married instead of taking this nonsensical position at Vox, which if discovered, will shame us all."

She paused and then went on:

"Can you imagine what they would say if they knew that George's niece was a common Governess?"

Marisa smiled.

"It might even lower his prestige in his Clubs," she said mockingly.

"It is not a joking matter," the Countess snapped. "For goodness sake go upstairs and change into the blue travelling gown that Rose has left out for you. I do not know why, but you look a complete houri in black, with that fiery hair of yours."

"I told you I should have dyed it," Marisa replied.

"Go away!" Lady Berrington said angrily. "You make me lose my temper, Marisa, and nothing is more calculated to give me lines on my forehead."

Marisa changed into a sapphire-blue dress with a matching mantle that had been left out for her in one of the upstairs bed-rooms.

There was a small hat to match and although she dragged back her hair, twisted it tightly into a chignon at the back of her head and covered it with a thick net, she had to admit when she was finally ready that no-one would guess from her appearance that she was what Lady Berrington had described as a "common Governess"!

She went downstairs to her aunt's room. Lady Berrington stared at her.

"The only thing I can say," she remarked, "is that it is fortunate there is no mistress at Vox. As I have told you before, no Lady in her senses would engage you as a governess for her children."

"Perhaps the Duke will not notice me," Marisa suggested.

"I am able to inform you that such a contingency is extremely unlikely!" Lady Berrington snorted. "The Duke is very occupied at the moment with Lady Wantage, although what he sees in that stupid, giggly creature, I cannot imagine."

"Lady Wantage," Marisa repeated reflectively. "Is she not one of 'The Professional Beauties'?"

The vogue of "The Professional Beauties" had been started in the 70's by Mrs. Lily Langtry.

Her example in posing for photographers who sold their pictures to an admiring public had been followed by Lady Randolph Churchill, Lady Dudley, Lady Helen Vincent and Mrs. Cornwallis-West.

A large section of society considered the publicity exceedingly vulgar and were shocked that "ladies" should lend themselves to such an outrageous fad.

It was part, they said of the undermining of Society and was entirely due to the influence of the Prince of Wales.

"I never admired Hetty Wantage myself," Lady Berrington said in a voice which told Marisa all too clearly that there was a great deal of emnity between the two.

"Well, if the Duke's affections are deeply engaged," Marisa said lightly, "you need not worry that he will turn his attention to me."

Lady Berrington laughed.

"You cannot seriously imagine that Valerius would lower himself to look at a governess?" she asked. "If you are going to Vox, Marisa, with the idea of capturing the most wealthy, the most important and the most elusive bachelor in the whole of the social world, you will be sadly disappointed."

"I certainly have no wish to capture the Duke, as you put it," Marisa replied. "In fact, as I have already told you, Aunt Kitty, although you will not believe me, I am not interested in men. I dislike them and I have no intention of ever being married."

"You would soon change your tune if you fell in love," Kitty Berrington said. "However with your Radical views it is very unlikely that any decent man would be so stupid as to fall in love with you."

"Then I am quite safe," Marisa smiled, "and anyway I assure you that love has no place in my plans for the future. If I have a heart, which I very much doubt, it is as frozen as an iceberg. It would require a volcanic eruption—much less a man—to melt it."

"Then you are certainly not like your mother," Lady Berrington remarked.

"In that respect no, I am not," Marisa agreed.

She thought now in the train how typical it was of her aunt and her friends to be obsessed by the thought of love and the pursuit of men. They had nothing else to do.

Marisa had learnt from Mrs. Featherstone-Haugh how it was, in fact, almost like a game, played with definite rules.

The Prince and his contemporaries never paid court to newly married women. That would have been considered in extremely bad taste and would certainly have caused a commotion.

Young wives in the Marlborough House Set were expected to behave circumspectly and produce children for their husbands for at least the first ten years of their married life.

After that, discreet and well-conducted love affairs were, in most cases, tolerated by their husbands unless they caused too much gossip.

The Duke, Marisa was sure, would behave according to the rules.

She was not quite certain how old Lady Wantage was, but she must be in her thirties and she remembered seeing post-cards of her on sale and thinking that her face, while lovely, had a somewhat insipid look about it.

It was important, Marisa thought, to get all the information she could.

If she was to lampoon the Duke really thoroughly in her book, she must find out every detail of his past love affairs and any which occupied him at the moment.

It should not be difficult, however discreet the great social figures might think themselves: someone always knew what was going on, someone invariably could be persuaded to talk.

Marisa chuckled to herself as she thought of the sheets and sheets of closely written manuscript which lay carefully packed in the bottom of a large leather bag which she carried herself.

It was locked, and while the servants could unpack the round-topped trunks provided for her by her aunt, she would take good care that no-one but herself had access to the leather bag.

The train had nearly reached the private Halt where trains would stop at the special request of guests for Vox Castle, before Marisa thought of the child she was to teach.

The little girl's education had been attempted by so many governesses, it was unlikely that she had learnt much. Marisa wondered whether it would have been wise to bring with her some simple lesson-books.

Then she realised it would be easy for her to ask for what she wanted, the Duke could hardly deny his daughter the most up-to-date publications that were suitable for children.

A closed carriage drawn by a pair of magnificent horseflesh waited for her outside the miniature Station with its complete toy-size Waiting Rooms.

There was a coachman and a footman on the box, and when Marisa sank back against the comfortable cushioned seat, she thought that at least the governess was met in style.

But she was well aware that, in the hierarchy of a great household, she was of very minor importance.

Vox took her breath away when she first saw it. She had known what to expect, but somehow it was more magnificent and more imposing than its pictures or photographs.

There was a great Norman tower on one side, then there was a profusion of roofs, chimneys and statues silhouetted against the sky and the Castle stood like a precious jewel against the deep green of its protective woods.

There were stone terraces and smooth lawns which stretched down to a lake fed by a stream that was crossed by several bridges.

There was a translucent glitter in the sunshine of hundreds of windows and the whole was so beautiful, so majestic, that Marisa could only stare at it as if spellbound.

Then the thought came to her mind that this fabulous Castle belonged to the man she hated. It was a pity, that its owner could not measure up to the loveliness of his possessions.

At the top of the stone steps leading up to a pillared front door, she was greeted by an elderly Butler and one of the half a dozen footmen in attendance was instructed to escort her upstairs.

"Miss Whitcham is expecting you, Miss Mitton," the Butler said.

There was just a touch of patronage in his voice which Marisa knew would not have been there had she had visited Vox under her own real name.

And she smiled to herself when the footman escorting her up the grand staircase chatted in a familiar manner.

"Did you have a good journey, Miss?" he asked. "I expect you came first class. It is all right for them that can afford it. I don't fancy travelling in one of them hard trucks. You looks like a chimney-sweep when you reach the other end."

"There is talk of them being improved," Marisa told him.

"Well until they are, I prefers to travel by coach," the footman replied. "Not that I often goes to London—too expensive for the likes of us—unless of course His Grace is paying."

He laughed as if it was a joke, then opening a door said in more respectful tones:

"The new governess, Miss."

Marisa entered and saw a middle-aged woman rise from a desk in a comfortable sitting-room which was however also fitted out as an office.

As Miss Whitcham moved towards her, Marisa saw that the Secretary was plump and grey-haired, plainly dressed in a serviceable tweed suit over a broderie Anglaise blouse.

She took her pince-nez from her nose and its chain slipped back into a little blue enamel container which she wore on her lapel as she said:

"How do you do, Miss Mitton, it is most obliging of you to come to us at such short notice."

"I was delighted to be free so that I could accommodate you," Marisa answered in what she hoped was a respectful yet ladylike manner.

"Please sit down," Miss Whitcham continued, indicating a chair.

She seated herself in one opposite.

"Lady Berrington spoke very highly of you," she began, "and of course, as Her Ladyship and new Earl are close friends of His Grace, that was all the recommendation I needed. The Duke is at the moment in Scotland and I am sure he would wish me to welcome you to Vox on his behalf."

Marisa said nothing and after a moment Miss Whitcham went on:

"You look very young. Can you really be twenty-four, which is the age Lady Berrington mentioned in her letter?"

"I have known Lady Berrington for many years," Marisa replied.

Miss Whitcham looked a little nervous and it seemed to Marisa almost as if she felt for the words as she continued:

"I think I should explain to you, Miss Mitton, that Lady Aline Verley, to give her her full title, is not a very easy child."

"I gathered from Lady Berrington that you had had quite a number of governesses," Marisa answered.

"Alas, that is true," Miss Whitcham said, "and Miss Graves whom you are replacing left hurriedly in, I regret to say, a quite hysterical state."

"Caused by Lady Aline?" Marisa asked.

"I am afraid so," Miss Whitcham admitted. "She is very unpredictable; in fact one is continually on edge wondering what she will do next."

"And what did she do to Miss Graves?" Marisa enquired.

She thought for a moment that Miss Whitcham was not going to reply, and then she said in a voice which sounded almost strangled with embarrassment:

"She put a snake in her bed!"

"How on earth did the child get hold of a snake?"

"It turned out to be a grass snake and quite harmless. But of course Miss Graves was not to know that. She had an aversion to reptiles. She told me she would not stay another night in the house, not if we offered her £100 a minute."

Marisa tried not to smile.

"I suppose Aline knew of Miss Graves' aversion."

"I should not be surprised," Miss Whitcham answered. "I will be quite frank with you, Miss Mitton, and say that I personally can do nothing with Aline. I have tried, I have talked to her as if I were her mother, but she is just rude and defiant. I can only hope with all my heart that you will succeed where others have failed."

"I will do my best," Marisa promised.

She thought to herself as she spoke that one advantage she had over the governesses who had come to Vox before, was that she anyway had no intention of staying very long.

In two to three months she would be able to finish her book.

Then if the advance that she expected was forthcoming, and she was supremely confident it would be, she would ask her Uncle to let her have a cottage on the Estate where she could live with her old governess who had retired years ago.

They would be very comfortable together and Miss Gillingham would love looking after her. She could write, and if she made the money she anticipated she would be able to travel.

Vox was only a stepping-stone to her ambition, and therefore Lady Aline's antics, whatever they might be, would merely be useful in showing how the younger generation in Society behaved. They certainly would not worry her unduly.

"I suppose in a way," Miss Whitcham was saying, "one should be sorry for the child. After all she has no mother and her father . . ."

She paused.

"Is the Duke fond of his daughter?" Marisa enquired.

Again there was a pause, until Miss Whitcham said almost reluctantly:

"It is only fair that you should know the truth, Miss Mitton. His Grace is not particularly interested in his daughter."

There was something in the way Miss Whitcham spoke which told Marisa quite clearly that the Secretary could say a great deal more if she wished to do so.

Miss Whitcham was a gossip, Marisa decided, and she knew that sooner or later it would be easy to persuade her to reveal whatever secrets there might be about the Duke and his relationship with his daughter.

But this was obviously not the moment. Miss Whitcham rose to her feet.

"I think," she said, "it would be best if you would come upstairs and meet Aline. Of course you only look after her during the day. Her old Nanny is still with her, and there is a housemaid and a footman to wait on the nurseries."

"That sounds comfortable!" Marisa smiled. "Tell me about the Nanny."

"She is very old and rather crotchety," Miss Whitcham replied in a low voice as she moved towards the door.

"She came to Vox with the late Duchess. She was not one of our hereditary staff."

She opened the door and added:

"I think I should explain there is a long tradition of families at Vox who have served the house and the estate one generation after another. Aline's Nurse is almost what we might term a foreigner, and so she has never got on with the other servants."

Marisa followed Miss Whitcham up another staircase to the second floor.

"My Sitting-room is here," Miss Whitcham said, "and I hope that you and I will have many cosy chats in it."

"Thank you," Marisa replied.

"The Nursery is up again," Miss Whitcham went on, starting up another staircase. "It is quite a climb, but as my mother always used to say, 'The higher you go, the nearer to Heaven'. That is something I have always remembered."

They reached the third floor and now Miss Whitcham opened a door into a large room into which the sunshine shone through two windows in a golden glow.

There was an old woman sitting beside a brightly burning fire, darning a sock. She rose as they entered, and Miss Whitcham raising her voice as if she was deaf said:

"Good afternoon, Nanny. I have brought the new governess, Miss Mitton, to meet Aline."

Marisa looked round and saw that on one wall there was an upright piano, while in another corner of the room there was a number of expensive toys.

There was a doll's house, a rocking-horse, a number of dolls and boxes of bricks all piled together neatly, which suggested that at least today no-one had played with them.

On a small table beside the toys was a large cardboard box.

The Nursery contained the traditional screen ornamented with transfers and Christmas cards. There was a guard in front of the fire and the brass rail shone in the light of the flames.

On the table in the centre of the room there was arranged a number of exercise-books, a bottle of ink and a pencil-box.

"I told Aline you were coming," the Nurse said to Marisa. "I put out her lesson books so you could see them. A nice mess they are."

"Where is Aline?" Miss Whitcham asked sharply.

"I think she's in her bed-room," Nanny replied. "She says she's sick of governesses."

The old woman moved across the room, opened a door at the far end and said coaxingly:

"Come along now, dearie. Don't be showing yourself at your worst when there's a nice young lady come all the way from London to teach you. You'd not have her thinking you're an ignoramus."

There was no response and Miss Whitcham said:

"That will be all, Nanny. I think you can leave me to talk to Aline."

"You'll be lucky if she attends to you," Marisa heard the Nurse say as she moved towards the door leading into the passage.

When she reached it she looked back. There was a faint smile on her wrinkled face, and Marisa had the impression that she was glad the child was difficult.

"I am sure she puts her against all the governesses," she thought. "It is understandable as Aline has been her baby up to now and she resents any other influence."

Miss Whitcham had gone to the bed-room door.

"Come along, Aline," she said, "if you do not come to say how do you do, I shall tell your father how rude you are, and you know how much he hates bad manners."

It seemed as if this was the magic formula, because almost instantly the child appeared.

She was dressed in a frilled muslin gown with a blue sash which somehow seemed too childish for her. She was tall for her age, well built, and she might have been attractive except that she was scowling to such an extent that her eye-brows almost met across her small nose.

She had dark hair which reached to her shoulders; her eyes were dark too and they seemed to Marisa, as they looked at her, to hold an expression not so much of dislike as of derision.

"Now, Aline," Whitcham said in the artificially jovial tone in which people so often spoke to children. "Here is Miss Mitton, I want you to say how do you do to her nicely."

Aline made no response and Miss Whitcham, as if to tide over an embarrassing moment, said quickly:

"You must show her all your toys and especially that lovely doll that Lady Wantage gave you last week. I see you have it here on the table. Oh dear, it makes me long to be young again, I never possessed such a beautiful doll myself!"

Aline made no move but stood scowling in the doorway as Miss Whitcham turned towards the big cardboard box which lay on the table amongst the toys.

"Dolls are so pretty these days," she said to Marisa, "and this one is hand-dressed. The clothes actually have real lace on them. Lady Wantage told me that it had come from Paris. Think of that, Aline, all the way from Paris!"

As she spoke she lifted the lid of the box, then gave a kind of stifled shriek.

Marisa, who had moved across the room automatically because she thought it was expected of her, stared down into the box.

There was no doubt the doll had originally been very expensive, but now its head was severed from its body, its face had been smashed in as if with a hammer and its pale pink dress, trimmed with real lace, had been slashed and cut into tatters.

"How could you? How could you do anything so naughty?" Miss Whitcham cried. "What will your father say after Lady Wantage had been so kind as to bring you such an expensive present?"

"I hate her!" Aline said hysterically. "I hate her and I hate the stupid doll which looks like her!"

"Really . . ." Miss Whitcham began.

Marisa stepped forward and taking the lid of the box from her hands, replaced it.

"I think," she said quietly, "it would be best if you left Aline and me alone so that we can get to know each other."

"Yes of course, if that is what you want," Miss Whitcham said obviously relieved. "All I can say, Aline, is that I am appalled by your behaviour! Quite appalled!"

She turned and went from the Nursery shutting the door behind her. Marisa took off her mantle and laid it on a chair, then she moved towards the fire.

Although the sun was shining outside, and the middle of the day was warm as so often happens in early September, there was a chill wind which she had felt as she walked down the platform.

Now she drew off her gloves and her bonnet and crossed the room to lay them both on top of her mantle.

Without looking at Aline she realised the child had moved to stand at one of the windows.

"I'm not going to do any lessons!" she said at length in a surly voice.

"Good!" Marisa replied. "That will give me more time to learn the things I want to learn."

There was silence until Aline said with a faint note of curiosity in her voice.

"But you're grown up—what do you want to learn?"

"So many things," Marisa answered. "First of all all the exciting stories there are attached to this Castle, and I want to hear the whole tale from the very beginning why a Roman senator built on this particular site and why he called it Vox."

"Everyone knows that silly old tale," Aline said rudely. "They asked him, if he built a fortress, how he could talk to the people in England and he said, 'This will be my voice!' "

"Yes but what was he supposed to talk to them about?" Marisa asked. "That is what I want to know. Do you think they were special magic things that he had come all the way from Rome to teach the English?"

She paused although she did not expect an answer. Then continued:

"I read somewhere that he was a man of mystery, a man who they looked on almost as a sorcerer!"

"I've never heard that," Aline said in a voice which still attempted to be rude.

"Well that is one of the things I want to learn," Marisa said, "and of course about the Normans who built an enormous Castle on the same site."

She moved across the room as she spoke to stand beside Aline looking out over the park towards the woods.

"And when I have explored this wonderful Castle with all its treasures," she said, "and discovered some of the very secret things which perhaps nobody else knows, then I want to explore the woods."

She paused for a moment and then she recited in a very low voice:

There is a special magic—night and day,
In woods—where dragons sleep and fairies play.

"Did you say . . . fairies?" Aline asked.

"Yes, I did," Marisa replied.

"Nanny says there's no such things as fairies."

"I think that is something everyone has to discover for himself," Marisa said. "I know I have seen dark green circles on the grass in the morning where I was sure little feet had danced the night before. I have seen mushrooms arranged as if they were seats at the foot of big fir trees. And when I have listened very carefully with my ear against the trunks of great oaks, I have been quite certain I have heard elves working away inside."

There was silence and then a small voice said:

"Are you going to—discover these—things—all by yourself?"

"You can come with me if you like," Marisa said casually, "but it does not matter if you are busy doing other things."

She turned from the window.

"What I want to do now," she said, "is to discover where I am sleeping and also to discover if they are bringing my trunks upstairs."

"I will show you," Aline said almost eagerly. "It is the room opposite this. It is quite nice, although Miss Graves did not like it because it looks over the front. She said the carriages kept her awake when Papa was entertaining."

"I should think it might be rather fun to see them," Marisa said. "Do you not think people have carriages that look just like themselves? Some are very grand and expensive, soft-cushioned and smart, and others are rackety old gigs with a very slow horse, and the men who own them are red faced, wear battered hats and smoke clay pipes."

Aline gave a little gurgle of laughter.

"Some people," she said, "look like horses."

"I have often thought that," Marisa agreed.

They had crossed the corridor by this time and Marisa saw that two of her round-topped boxes had been brought upstairs. There were two more to come, for Aunt Kitty had been extremely generous.

A fresh-faced housemaid was pulling back the lids on the ones that were there already. A footman had already undone the straps.

"Shall I unpack for you, Miss?" she asked.

"Thank you," Marisa replied.

She put down her cape and bonnet, and then looking at Aline she said:

"I think we have time to make a few discoveries before tea. Would you like to show me the rooms downstairs?"

It was an hour later before they came back to the Nursery.

In that time Marisa had seen quite a lot of the great house. The long Picture Gallery with its wonderful collection of Van Dykes, the Salons which contained magnificent valuable furniture, and the Library which made her give a cry of sheer delight.

"It is only a lot of old books!" Aline said.

She was still attempting, though rather ineffectively, to show no enthusiasm for what obviously thrilled Marisa.

"Books!" Marisa exclaimed. "Oh, Aline, think how exciting they are! Think of the very special secrets they all contain. Things we want to know! Things we want to find out!"

"What sort of secrets?" Aline enquired.

"Every sort of secret," Marisa replied. "If you want to know about fairies, for instance, I can find you stories about them, poems about them and descriptions of them. And if we search very hard, we might even find pictures of them!"

"Can we really?" Aline asked. "Nobody ever told me that before."

"Perhaps they did not want you to know," Marisa said.

This, as she had intended, made Aline determined immediately not to be excluded from something that might interest her.

"Let us go and search now," she suggested.

"It is going to be a big task until we can find our way about," Marisa replied.

Marisa knew she had been handed the key to Aline's character. The child loved her father and she was jealous of the women in whom he was interested.

"Do you know what my grandfather used to do when he hated anyone?" Marisa asked.

Aline looked at her with stormy eyes and she went on:

"He used to write their name on a piece of paper and then he used to put it away in a drawer in his desk. He said that prevented him from thinking about them and hating them, which he thought unlucky. Ten years later, when he looked in the drawer, he could not remember who they were or why he had written down their names."

"Was it magic?" Aline asked.

"A sort of magic," Marisa replied "You see, when you hate someone you send out an invisible dagger towards them. You think it is going to hurt them, but if they have a special magic of their own to protect them, then the dagger turns round and stabs you. That is true magic, I promise you."

Aline stared at her a long time and then she said:

"And if you love somebody what happens?"

This was something Marisa had never considered, but after a moment she replied:

"I think love is something nice which everyone wants and so they would keep it."

After a moment she added:

"You love your Papa, do you not?"

"I love him and he loves me—he does—he does!" Aline cried.

There was so much passion in her voice that Marisa was surprised.

"Nanny says that he does not love anyone but himself," the child went on, "but he loves me, I know he does!"

Aline jumped up from the table as she spoke and Marisa knew it was to hide the tears that had suddenly sprung to her eyes.

Wisely she changed the conversation.

That evening after Aline had gone to bed, Marisa went down to Miss Whitcham's Sitting-room.

It was warm and cosy, filled with little knick-knacks, presents from abroad and souvenirs that Miss Whitcham

had collected for years. She had even kept every Christmas card the Duchess had ever given her.

"Tomorrow," Miss Whitcham said, "I hope you will
dine with me here rather than upstairs. I did not like to
suggest it this evening in case you were too busy settling
in, but I feel, Miss Mitton, that we are going to be friends.
I do not mind telling you that some times I am very
lonely."

"I am sure you are," Marisa agreed.

"Of course I am always busy," Miss Whitcham went
on. "The Duke relies on me entirely to run the social side
of the Castle. It is I who decide what bed-rooms the
guests will have, and that is quite a headache on its own, I
can assure you."

"Why?" Marisa asked.

Miss Whitcham looked a little coy.

"Well you do understand, Miss Mitton, it is very important how people are placed. If the Duchess of Man-
chester for instance wishes to be near a certain handsome
gentleman with whom she is having a very discreet flirtation, she would be extremely annoyed to find he had been
placed on another floor!"

"Oh! I do see that requires a great deal of diplomacy,"
Marisa smiled.

"I often think of myself as 'The Discreet Custodian',"
Miss Whitcham continued. "I assure you, Miss Mitton,
there is very little that goes on in this house of what I am
not aware, but naturally I keep such knowledge to myself."

"Of course," Marisa agreed knowing it was untrue and
Miss Whitcham was an inveterate gossip.

"His Grace knows that I will supervise everything,"
Miss Whitcham continued. "Can you believe that I was
told the other day that the blotting-paper was not changed
in the bed-room of one of our famous Ducal houses? With
the result that the next guest read a most loving letter that
had been written to her own husband by a lady who of
course must be nameless!"

"How frightening that such a little omission could cause
so much trouble," Marisa exclaimed.

"It very nearly became a *Cause Célèbre*," Miss Whitcham replied in an excruciating French accent. "And

that is why I need a dozen eyes in my head. After all the Duke trusts me."

"And very wisely I am sure," Marisa said. "Whatever would he do if you were not here?"

"I often wonder myself," Miss Whitcham replied. "And his mother before she died often remarked, 'I cannot think what we would do without you, Whitchy.' It was the Duchess' pet name for me."

"Aline is very fond of her father," Marisa remarked.

"Indeed! Did she tell you so?" Miss Whitcham enquired.

"Yes she told me that she loves him."

"I can't think why," Miss Whitcham ejaculated almost without thinking. "He pays little enough attention to her."

"Perhaps he could be persuaded to show her more affection," Marisa remarked.

Miss Whitcham looked absolutely horrified.

"Oh, you cannot suggest such a thing to His Grace! I beg you not to mention anything like that, Miss Mitton. It would be unthinkable!"

"But why?" Marisa enquired. "After all the child has no mother. The Duke must realise that it is quite natural for her to turn to him for the love and sense of security that every child seeks from its parents."

Miss Whitcham looked agitated.

"You put me in a difficult position, Miss Mitton," she said at length. "I realise that you have a very hard task in front of you in trying to teach Aline, and yet, though it seems a strange thing to say, though you appear so young, there is something about you different from the other governesses I have engaged on His Grace's behalf. You may think it presumptious on such a short acquaintance, yet I cannot help telling you, that already I have confidence in you."

"Then I hope you will help me," Marisa said. "Tell me why I may not suggest to the Duke that he gives his only child the affection she obviously craves from him."

"I suppose really I ought not to tell you," Miss Whitcham said uneasily, "though you might easily hear it from one of the servants, or from that gossiping old Nanny. The fact is, Miss Mitton . . ."

She paused.

"Please go on," Marisa pleaded.

"Well, you doubtless know the late Duchess was very neurotic, in fact it seems as though at times she was not in full possession of her faculties. She took a pleasure in upsetting her husband, it often happens I believe when people are slightly deranged, that they appear to hate the people who do the most for them. Anyway she tried in every way possible to annoy and to hurt him."

"What did she do in particular?" Marisa asked.

"She told His Grace," Miss Whitcham answered almost in a whisper, "the child was not his."

Chapter Three

The Duke of Milverley stepped onto the platform at St. Pancras Station in a bad temper.

He had travelled down from Dunrobin Castle in Scotland in the Prince of Wales' private train on which the Royal footmen had served a superb meal, and the guests were called in the morning with the early newspapers picked up at Crewe.

The gentlemen in the party had played Bridge until the early hours of the morning which might have accounted for the Duke feeling not in his best form, had there not also been something specific to cause him anxiety.

The Duke of Sutherland's shooting party at Dunrobin Castle had included the Prince of Wales who had come on there from Balmoral.

Princess Alexandra and the two princesses, Victoria and Maude, were visiting Denmark, and His Royal Highness had, as usual, enjoyed the company of the beautiful women who were invited to entertain his guests.

Among them it was not surprising to find the fascinating Lady Brooke with whom the Prince had been obviously and deeply enamoured for the last two years.

Daisy Brooke, who had turned to His Royal Highness for help regarding an indiscreet letter, had not only captured the Prince's heart, but had found that she had begun to reciprocate his affections.

Lady Brooke was beautiful and she had a fascination which enthralled everyone, male or female, who came in contact with her.

Even her very staid relations and the more strait-laced

and disapproving of London hostesses found that they could not help loving Daisy despite the fact that they deprecated many of the things she did.

As the Duke of Milverley had been one of the guests at Dunrobin Castle, it was obvious that Lord and Lady Wantage should be invited also.

It was the first time that Lady Wantage had stayed in the fairy-tale Castle, with its towers and turrets, standing high above the sea with magnificent formal gardens embellished with fountains which reminded the beholders of Versailles.

Hetty Wantage admired everything and the Duke found her enthusiasm rather touching.

What was more, the pink and white of her complexion, the fairness of her were enhanced by the Highland air, and she looked ravishing in a tartan.

But after three days at Dunrobin Castle, Hetty had taken the Duke aside and told him that Lord Wantage was being difficult.

"What do you mean difficult?" the Duke enquired.

"He is jealous, Valerius," Hetty replied. "As I have told you before, in the eleven years that we have been married, I have never before looked at anyone else and Bernard does not like it."

"Is he suspicious?" the Duke enquired.

Hetty shrugged her shoulders.

It was a little mannerism she had adopted from the French and she knew it drew attention to her white shoulders and her long swan-like neck.

"We must be careful," the Duke said firmly.

"Yes, of course, we must be very careful," Hetty agreed, and her large blue eyes seemed to fill with tears.

"Oh Valerius! I cannot, I cannot give you up!"

"There is no question of that," the Duke replied in his deep voice. "We must just do our best not to draw attention to ourselves, and, for goodness sake, be charming to your husband."

He knew from experience that the danger with many women was that once they were in love they neglected their husbands or even positively showed their distaste for them.

The Duke would have been a fool, which he was not, had he not realised that his fascination for women lay a great deal in the fact that he did not find them absolutely essential to him.

He had many other things to occupy his mind and, unlike many of his contemporaries, did not waste his brain, his time and his energy entirely in pursuit of the fair sex.

He was of course well aware of his attractions and his own consequence.

He had no intention of ever again being inveigled into marriage with some half-witted girl who wished to wear the Milverley diamonds.

He had, since the death of his wife, had a number of discreetly conducted, but extremely entertaining love affairs with married women, whose husbands had most conveniently turned a blind eye to what was taking place.

He had not thought that Lord Wantage had noticed or would indeed object if he paid court to the delectable Hetty.

Bernard Wantage was a strong character. He was what the Duke thought of as a "calculated eccentric."

He dressed in an exaggerated style, he sported an enormous moustache which was the delight of cartoonists and which had made his face familiar to the man in the street.

Lord Wantage was extremely popular on race-courses, not only because his horses won, but because in the view of the ordinary public he was their ideal of a sportsman.

With his top-hat at a rakish angle, his moustache shooting out three inches on either side of his face, he drew attention whenever he appeared.

He always wore a yellow carnation, his racing colours were yellow, and his carriages and his servants livery were were in yellow and black.

He had been nick-named "Waspie Wantage," and now the Duke wondered if the name had a greater significance than the fact that his vehicles resembled the insect with an unpleasant sting in its tail.

Although the Duke was younger than the Prince of Wales, they were close friends and the Duke had no desire to cause a scandal which would react immediately on Marlborough House.

At the moment everyone who was fond of the Prince was trying to play down the public criticism and the aggressive newspaper articles arising from the Tanbury Croft case which had infuriated Queen Victoria and which, as she wrote to her son, "had brought the whole monarchy into disrepute."

Cheating was not only bad form, but it was something that even the man in the street realised was unsportsmanlike.

That Sir William Gordon Canning had dared to bring a libel action which involved the Prince of Wales against those who had accused him of cheating at baccarat, caused so much comment that, whatever way the trial had gone, there was no question that some of the mud which had been thrown during the hearings was bound to stick.

Sir William was finally dismissed from the Army and expelled from all his Clubs, but it was on the Prince of Wales that the country showered its indignation.

"The press have been particularly severe and cruel because they know I cannot defend myself," the Prince had said to the Duke.

There was nothing His Grace could reply except to hope, as in every other scandal, time would bring forgetfulness.

But against this background the Duke knew that, if Lord Wantage were to turn nasty, things could be very difficult indeed.

He lay awake as the train thundered through the night, knowing that if he was wise he would tell Lady Wantage it would be best for them not to meet again except in public, at any rate until Lord Wantage's suspicions were laid to rest.

It was hard to know what Lord Wantage's feelings were.

At Dunrobin Castle he was as amusing as always. He told the usual somewhat indecent stories after dinner. He shot well, lost at cards with good grace, and altogether behaved in a quite exemplary manner.

If the Duke felt there was a certain coldness when they spoke to each other, it was not perceptible enough for him to be certain that it was not his imagination.

"I should have give her up," he told himself.

Then some obstinacy within him asked:

"Why the devil should I? She attracts me and she undoubtedly fancies herself in love with me."

Those misty blue eyes, half swimming with tears, could be very alluring. The Duke liked feminine women, they gave him a feeling of superiority and strength.

In fact all his love affairs had been with women who clung to him and murmured protestations of love, to which he responded a little in the manner of a Sultan accepting a tribute from one of his concubines.

He thanked God as he said goodbye to the Prince and the house-party at St. Pancras Station that he himself was not overwhelmingly in love.

He had sworn after his experiences with Lady de Grey, that he would never really fall in love again, and he had kept his vow.

He could be amused, infatuated, even slightly captivated, but at the back of his brain a cold, calculating part of himself stood back and watched.

Never again, he thought, would he be a vulnerable love-sick youth and walk the streets at night because he could not sleep.

He could remember the hours he had stood outside a certain house in Berkeley Square in silent homage to the woman he loved!

He could recall all too vividly being swept into a delirium of delight by a kind word or a smile from two red lips, or cast into a hell of despondency.

He would be sorry to give up Hetty Wantage, but if her husband was going to be tiresome, it would be the only thing to do.

He would make the decision, he thought, after the week-end when they were coming to stay at Vox.

The Prince had intimated that he would like to come to the Castle the next day and stay until Monday. On Tuesday Princess Alexandra would return from abroad.

The Duke of course knew whom he was expected to ask, and Lord and Lady Brooke were among his guests.

"Let us be a small party on Thursday night," the Prince had suggested.

"A good idea, Sir," the Duke replied.

"The rest can arrive on Friday and will doubtless wish to shoot your partridges on Saturday," the Prince continued.

"It will all be arranged, Sir," the Duke promised.

He had decided that he would go straight to Vox on arriving at London rather than stay the night at Milverley House in Grosvenor Square.

Even at such short notice, a special reserved compartment was found for him on the train from Sussex, another carriage contained his Courier who always travelled with him, his valet and two footmen.

There was also a Secretary who had joined the party on hearing that His Grace was passing straight through London, and had brought all the letters that had been waiting his arrival at Milverley House.

The Duke made no effort to read the large pile of newspapers that had been laid beside him or even to sample the luncheon in a special basket marked with the Ducal Crown, that had been provided at a moment's notice by his London Chef.

He noted with an air almost of distaste the pâté, the quail in aspic, the lamb cutlets and the large hot-house peaches that had travelled to London from the greenhouse at Vox.

He did however pour himself out a glass of champagne and lying back against the seat stared with unseeing eyes at the landscape moving swiftly past.

He was thinking of the warmth and softness of Hetty Wantage's body and the impulsive manner in which she would throw her arms round his neck whenever they were alone together.

Her face would light up when he appeared in her Drawing-room and they had been closeted together alone on several afternoons before they went to Scotland while Lord Wantage was at his Club.

Hetty was not perhaps as strictly beautiful as some of the other women on whom the Duke had bestowed his attentions.

But he found her fascinating and was loath to part with

anything quite so delectable, specially because he felt that to draw back was to brand himself as a coward.

"Damn it, Wantage should behave in a more civilised manner!" the Duke said aloud.

He was sure that, were the position reversed, he would not object to his wife's philanderings, so long as they were not too obvious.

The Duke was so intent on his thoughts that the train reached the Halt for Vox Castle with his letters still unopened and the newspapers unfolded.

His carriage with a coachman and two footmen was waiting and while the Courier was left to see to the luggage, the guns, and all the paraphernalia which had been brought from Scotland, the Duke drove away.

As always, the sight of Vox exerted a soothing effect on him.

It was so beautiful, so much a part of himself, he could never return home without feeling a warm satisfaction at its perfection.

The leaves were beginning to fall from the trees, the oaks were russet brown, and the late September wind had a sharpness in it that was exhilarating.

"Welcome home, Your Grace," the Butler said bowing as the Duke entered the great Hall.

"Order Samson, I will change and go riding," the Duke replied.

"Very good, Your Grace."

The Duke went up the stairs in a hurry almost like a boy who was looking forward to his holidays.

He had a sudden desire to be out in the sunshine, to feel the wind on his face and forget everything except Vox itself.

When he returned he would see Miss Whitcham about the arrangements for the house-party, send for the gamekeeper and decide which were the best beats on which to take his guests on Saturday.

In the meantime the thought of riding Samson, a stallion he had only recently purchased, was a pleasure in itself.

Once mounted, the Duke galloped the horse to take the

freshness out of him, then riding across the park made for the woods.

There was some ground at the North end of the estate that he had not visited for some time and which he thought might have a better supply of partridges than the nearer beats that were shot over more often.

He wanted to go and look for himself, and he wended his way through the woods, his horse moving almost silently over the fallen leaves and the pine needles which bestrewed the mossy paths which were so seldom used.

The Duke came out of the darkness of the trees and was moving through some undergrowth, when he heard a shot ahead of him.

He wondered what it could be, and the thought of poachers coming into his mind he quickened the pace of his horse.

Then just ahead of him above the undergrowth, which was about the height of Samson, he saw a pheasant rise.

"Do not shoot!" he heard a woman's voice cry.

But with the words there came the sound of a shot and the Duke saw the bird stagger in the air.

"I hit it! I hit it!" a child's voice shouted before the woman said:

"It is wounded!"

The bird, obviously hit, was winging its way into the distance when another shot rang out.

With what the Duke knew was superb marksmanship, the bird was hit in the beak, crumpled up and fell like a stone to the ground.

There was a cry of delight.

"It is dead! It is dead!"

The Duke emerged from the undergrowth and saw first a child, whom he recognised as his daughter, running across a ploughed field apparently to retrieve the dead bird.

Standing with a gun in her hands was a woman. The Duke turned on her furiously:

"Who are you?" he demanded. "And what the devil do you mean by shooting my pheasants out of season?"

As his voice rang out with the violence of his feelings,

the woman turned to face him and he found himself looking down into two very large green eyes.

For a moment they obviously questioned who he might be, before he saw recognition dawn in her expression and then to his surprise be replaced with a look that he could only feel was one of hostility, if not active dislike.

There was a pause until quietly in a musical voice with a dignity that he had not expected the woman said:

"I am Aline's new governess, Your Grace. My name is Mitton."

"New governess!" the Duke ejaculated. "And do you consider, Miss Mitton, that shooting is an essential part of a girl's education?"

"It teaches accuracy, quickness of judgement and balance," was the answer.

The Duke was about to reply when he saw that the governess was watching Aline pick up the bird and turn to come back with it. She looked up again at the Duke.

"Tell Aline it was a good shot!" she urged. "It is important that you should commend her."

There was so much insistence in her voice that the Duke was astonished into silence.

Never had he expected a governess to tell him what to do, and certainly not in a tone that was almost a command.

"I think, Miss Mitton . . ." he began only to be interrupted as he realised that Aline had seen him and was running excitedly over the plough holding the pheasant by the legs.

"I shot it, Papa, I shot it! Did you see me?"

"I saw you," the Duke said and the words were grim.

He perceived that his daughter was carrying under her arm a small gun that he himself had used at the same age.

It somehow moderated the scathing remarks he was about to make to Miss Mitton, and as Aline reached the side of his horse and stood holding up the pheasant, her cheeks flushed, her eyes excited, he found it hard to be as censorious as he had intended.

"It is dead, Papa, I shot it!"

"With a little help from your companion," the Duke remarked dryly.

"It is difficult to kill a pheasant with such a small gun," Miss Mitton said.

She made it a statement of fact.

"I can shoot, Papa! I have already shot a pigeon," Aline told him, "and I think I hit a rabbit, but we could not find it."

As she spoke one of the under-keepers came out of the wood with his dog.

Over his shoulder he carried a stick on which was hung quite an assortment of game. There were half a dozen pigeons, two magpies, a carrion crow, a jay and three rabbits.

"The Head Keeper gave us permission, Your Grace, to shoot vermin," Marisa said in explanation.

"Quite a bag, Miss Mitton!" the Duke said, a sarcastic note in his voice.

"The pheasant of course was a mistake," Marisa said. "I think Aline was a little excited, otherwise we are both aware that they are not in season until next week."

"I am relieved to hear that you have such extensive knowledge of sport," the Duke said, again in a sarcastic tone he had used before.

"It was clever of me, was it not, Papa?" Aline continued, still holding her pheasant by the hand and looking up at the Duke almost pleadingly.

"You certainly hit it, Aline," the Duke replied.

Then he turned his horse and rode back into the wood, the way he had come.

Aline stood looking after him and there was something so forlorn in her attitude that Marisa said quickly:

"He thought it a very good shot, Aline."

"He did not say so," Aline answered and her voice trembled.

"I think he was rather surprised to see us," Marisa answered. "You see, Aline, if you had been a boy your father would have expected to find you out shooting, but he has to get used to the idea of a girl doing such things."

"If I had been a boy he would have said it was very good," Aline remarked.

"Of course he would, because it was good!" Marisa agreed. "But, Aline, you have to realise that men expect us women to sit about all day sewing a sampler or paint-

ing little water colours. You and I have to educate your
father into realizing we want to do something different."

The sparkle came back into Aline's eyes.

"Shall we be able to educate him?" she asked.

"We will have a good try," Marisa assured her. "Now
give Scott your pheasant. I think we must find the
pony-cart and drive back to the Castle. I did not know
your father was coming today."

She wondered as they returned whether the Duke
would forbid Aline to go shooting again.

She was hoping that she could persuade him not to do
so, although after hearing the anger in his voice and
seeing the somewhat grim expression on his face, she was
apprehensive of what the future might hold.

She had known that she would hate the Duke when she
saw him.

She had felt, even amongst the beauty and peace of
Vox, that his presence was there, disturbing her and in a
way threatening her. But she had also thought she knew
what he looked like.

It had not been the same as seeing him in person.

She had not expected him to be quite so big, quite so
over-powering. He was overwhelmingly omnipotent, she
thought, the kind of man one imagined Alexander the
Great had been, or Hannibal driving his elephants over
the Alps.

Even to look at the Duke she could feel that he was a
fighter and a commander, a man who would not bow to
expediency, or even to reason unless it pleased him to do
so.

As she and Aline drove back in silence towards the
Castle, she told herself that the Duke was even worse than
she had anticipated.

She felt suddenly frantic that he might undo all the
good she had done for Aline since she had come to Vox.

She had been at the Castle for almost three weeks and
she had made so many changes that it was stupid not to
realise that the Duke might find them unacceptable.

Marisa had been appalled to discover what a restricted,
unhappy life Aline was leading.

In the first place she had little exercise. Her previous
governesses had disliked walking. The child was taken out

riding on a lazy fat pony with a groom on a leading-rein three times a week.

Otherwise she kicked her heels round the Nursery being given no incentive to use either her brain or her imagination, and having no real attention paid to her except being injudiciously fed and continually admonished to behave herself.

The food was well cooked, but it was what the Chef considered proper nursery fare.

Lots of stodgy puddings, too much white bread and butter and sugary cakes, very little fruit although the greenhouses were groaning with peaches and grapes, and not enough green vegetables.

The fact that Aline had spots on her face was a sure sign that her food was disagreeing with her.

Marisa asked that she might work out the menus with the Chef and Miss Whitcham, although at first protesting it had never been done before, gave in with quite a good grace.

Marisa, who was extremely fond of riding, insisted that she and Aline ride every morning for at least two hours and in the afternoon they would walk for miles.

They explored the woods as she had promised Aline they would do, finding strange things the child had never seen before while she learnt about trees, shrubs and flowers.

Marisa was horrified that no governess had ever bothered to teach Aline the difference between an oak and an ash tree.

No governess had explained the herbs in the herb-garden or told the child of their uses. No governess had ever dug with their charge in a sand-bank which they discovered among the pine trees beyond the shrubberies.

It was here that they buried surreptitiously the battered doll which Lady Wantage had given Aline. She enjoyed the secrecy and the excitement of making a hole deep enough to cover the toy.

It delighted Marisa to see the colour come back in Aline's face and to see how seldom she now scowled.

She found she was gaining the child's confidence and in consequence Aline was gradually becoming easy to handle. When she flew into a tantrum, as she still did when she could not get her own way, Marisa would walk out of the room.

Ten minutes later there would be a knock on her door and Aline would apologise.

Once when she had been particularly naughty, Marisa went for a walk in the garden. It was half an hour before a hot little hand was slipped into hers and a frightened voice said:

"I could not find you ... I was afraid you had gone away!"

"I do not know what you have done to that child," Miss Whitcham remarked, "but she is certainly different from what she used to be. You really are a miracle-worker, Miss Mitton!"

"I would rather call it using common sense," Marisa had answered.

She was in fact furiously resentful at the manner in which Aline had been allowed to get out of hand and had been decried affection and proper consideration. She blamed the Duke.

Back at the Castle they had tea. There was a boiled egg for Aline and a big bowl of fruit stood on the table. There were also tomato sandwiches made with home-made brown bread and a watercress salad.

"Do you think, Papa will want to see me?" Aline asked.

"Perhaps he will be too busy this evening," Marisa answered and her lips tightened when she saw the disappointment in Aline's eyes.

Nanny, grumbling and as spiteful and crotchety as she dared to Marisa, had put the little girl to bed before a footman came to the School-room door.

"His Grace would like to speak to you, Miss, in the Study."

Marisa knew as he spoke she had been anticipating such a summons.

Just for a moment she felt afraid. Astride the big black stallion the Duke had been majestic and awe-inspiring.

Then she told herself with a little lift of her chin she was not afraid of anyone. After all what had she to fear? At worst the Duke could dismiss her.

Anyway she did not intend to stay very long at the Castle.

It would however be annoying if he sent her away immediately, for she had been so busy and concerned with Aline that she had found there was very little time to think of her book.

She had, it was true, gone down to the Library almost every evening after supper with Miss Whitcham.

But the multitudinous choice of literature had proved so interesting and so tempting that instead of carrying out the research she needed for her own writing, she found herself immersed in the latest editions of books of which she had heard, but never had the chance to read.

She approached the Duke's Study, where she had learnt that he habitually sat, with her head held high and with a feeling that for Aline's sake, as well as for her own, she must not be too provocative.

The Study over-looked the lake and the sun was sinking in a blaze of glory behind the pine trees, bringing a golden glow to the room. It made the Duke as he turned from the window seem to come towards Marisa in a burst of fire.

She stood just inside the door.

Her hair was vividly red against the dark panelling and belied the severity of the plain dark-green gown that she had chosen particularly because, with its white collar and cuffs, it had almost a puritan air.

Lady Berrington had bought it much decorated with an elaborate amount of expensive lace, but Marisa had removed this as she felt it was too ostentatious for a governess.

However there was nothing she could do to prevent the colour accentuating the whiteness of her skin or hide the fact that her green eyes were angry but at the same time a little apprehensive.

"Come in, Miss Mitton," the Duke said, "I wish to talk with you."

He seated himself in the high-backed chair behind his desk and indicated a chair on the other side.

He looked extremely elegant, his clothes were by no means exaggerated and yet exquisitely cut and he wore them as if they were incidental and not of particular importance to him.

And yet Marisa thought there was something arrogant in the manner he lay back in his chair and the manner in which his grey eyes seemed to take in every detail of her appearance.

She felt they looked deep into her very soul as if he were searching for something. But what it might be she had no idea.

She only felt as if he might guess that she was not what she pretended to be. Then she told herself she was just being fanciful!

The Duke was nothing but a dilettante, a man without scruples or morals who was prepared to waste his life making love to other men's wives and to neglect a child.

Yet Marisa had to admit he was devastatingly handsome despite the cynical lines on his face, the twist of his lips and the indolent droop of his eyelids.

Moreover, much as she disliked him, it was impossible not to be pulsatingly aware of him.

It infuriated her to feel so disturbed in his presence. And she knew that despite her resolution to appear indifferent to anything he might say, her heart was beating unaccountably in her breast.

There was a silence which made her raise her chin. Finally the Duke said:

"I should be interested, Miss Mitton, to hear your opinion of my daughter. I am afraid the other governesses I have employed have been somewhat uncomplimentary about her intelligence. Is she so stupid?"

"On the contrary, I find Aline has an exceptionally quick brain," Marisa answered. "She has a retentive memory and an imagination that she has never been encouraged to exercise. But she is, in my opinion, one of the most neglected children I have ever encountered."

"Neglected!"

If Marisa had meant to surprise the Duke, she had certainly succeeded. He sat up in his chair and glared at her across the desk.

"What do you mean neglected? Surely there are enough people to look after her?"

"There is her old Nurse," Marisa replied, "who is too old to be in charge of children and should have been retired years ago. She is quite obstinately determined that no-one shall influence Aline but herself. She makes the child aggressive and fills her head with a lot of nonsense.

A governess has little chance of being successful as long as Nanny is with Aline."

Marisa paused a moment to let her words sink in and then she went on:

"The other people who look after Aline are of course servants. They gossip and talk in front of her as if she were not there. It is a habit not confined to the servant class, as Your Grace must know."

"You are certainly frank, Miss Mitton," the Duke said. "May I ask your suggestions on how to improve Aline's well-being?"

"I intended to ask you as soon as you returned home," Marisa answered, "if there were not some children on the Estate of about the same age. Can you imagine what it is like for a child of Aline's age to have no companions with whom she can play and laugh?"

She paused before continuing—

"She has in fact been brought up in very much the same way as the Prince of Wales, who, I understand, was never allowed the companionship of other boys. When other children came to tea, the Queen and the Prince Consort were always present."

"At least I do not err in that direction," the Duke remarked.

"And yet it is the one thing that would help Aline," Marisa answered.

She would have said more, but the Duke interrupted.

"I am told by Miss Whitcham that Aline smashed a very expensive doll that was given her by one of my friends. I intend to speak to her about it, but perhaps you have already punished her for such an unaccountable misdemeanour."

"No, I have not punished her," Marisa replied, "but we have buried the evidence of the crime."

"Buried!" the Duke ejaculated and just for a moment she thought there was a twinkle in his eye. "But why do you think she indulged in such behaviour?"

"Because she is jealous," Marisa answered.

"Jealous?" the Duke questioned.

"Of you."

"But that is absurd!"

"Do you really think so?" Marisa enquired. "After all it

is quite understandable. Seeing no-one except servants, all
her interest is centred on you. It is usual for small girls to
adore their fathers. I adored mine. But with Aline it is an
obsession. She therefore, and surely it is understandable,
dislikes anyone who gains your attention or who she
thinks wishes to do so."

The Duke rose from the desk and walked across the
room towards the window.

"I can hardly credit that you are telling me the truth,
Miss Mitton," he said.

"Please try to believe me," Marisa pleaded. "If only you
would be a little kind to Aline, if only you would encourage her and let her show you some affection, I assure you
she would become a perfectly normal and very charming
child."

The Duke did not reply but stood staring out at the
sunset. After a moment he said slowly:

"You have certainly given me something to think
about, Miss Mitton. In the meantime do you intend to
continue teaching my daughter to shoot? I should have
thought she was much too young."

"You learnt at the same age," Marisa said.

"I was a boy."

"You were also a child," Marisa replied, "you wanted
the interest, the excitement and the exercise."

"It is not a particularly feminine accomplishment," the
Duke said.

"Aline is not the type of little girl to be interested in
needlework or painting pretty water colours!" Marisa said
with a sharp note in her voice. "Besides I have never been
convinced that such qualifications make one a better,
wiser or more charming woman."

The Duke turned from the window.

"I am beginning to be afraid, Miss Mitton, that you are
one of the New Women that I have been reading about in
the newspapers. With all these strange and rather revolutionary ideas you are introducing into the School-Room, I
can only hope your politics are not equally disruptive."

"I will try not to include my political views in Aline's
curriculum," Marisa answered demurely.

"By that I infer that your views are not the same as
mine," the Duke said.

There was silence and he walked back to the desk to sit down again facing her.

"Let me tell you quite frankly, Miss Mitton," he said, "that I am disturbed by your ideas, but at the same time I have heard from Miss Whitcham of the tremendous improvement that Aline has made since you have come to the Castle. I am of course grateful for that. May I think over what you have suggested about having other children to be taught with her? Perhaps we can discuss it again before I leave for London next week."

Marisa rose to her feet.

"I thank Your Grace, I shall look forward to hearing from you."

The Duke too had risen. Then as she turned towards the door he said in a different tone:

"Who are you? Where do you come from?"

"I was recommended by Lady Berrington, Your Grace. She has known me for some years."

"And your home?"

"It is in Hertfordshire."

"Are your parents alive?"

"No, Your Grace, they are both dead."

"So that is why you are having to earn your own living. You do not look like an ordinary governess, Miss Mitton."

"That is, of course, my misfortune."

"I think most people would say you are very fortunate in your appearance," the Duke said gravely.

There was a hint of mischief in Marisa's eyes as she replied:

"I have been warned, Your Grace, that it might prove a considerable disadvantage, should I be interviewed by the lady of a house."

"Perhaps it was fortunate that I was not at home when you arrived," the Duke replied with a smile.

"Are you suggesting, Your Grace, that you would not have permitted me to enter your household?"

"I was suggesting nothing of the sort!" the Duke answered. "I am merely surprised, Miss Mitton, that someone as attractive as yourself cannot find a more congenial position."

"I assure you, Your Grace, I find it extremely congenial. There is so much beauty here and so much to learn that I feel breathless whenever I look around me."

She made a little gesture with her hand and went on.

"Do you realise that no-one had ever attempted to tell Aline the story of her heritage, or explain the history of the books, the furniture, or any of the other lovely things these rooms hold?"

"I am wondering how you are so knowledgeable," the Duke said. "Can you have studied so much in your very short life?"

"I am still learning, Your Grace."

"And so am I," he answered. "Perhaps there are some things we might even teach each other."

He spoke casually enough, but when Marisa looked up her eyes were caught by the expression in his.

There was something in their dark depth which made her feel suddenly breathless. The glow of the sunset filling the Library turned her hair into a shining glory.

It was almost as if they stood still and the world stood still with them; as if they met, not for the first time, but across eternity.

Then Marisa's eyes fell, her lashes dark against the transparency of her skin.

"I thank you, Your Grace, for listening to me," she said in an almost inaudible voice.

Then she moved to the door, opened it and went out.

Chapter Four

". . . then there was the Marchioness of Paddington," Miss Whitcham continued. "She was pretty and looked very smart in the hunting field. She stabled her horses here all one winter. We all grew fond of her and of course she literally worshipped the ground the Duke walked on."

Marisa had wanted to learn about the Duke's various infatuations but now, for some reason she could not explain even to herself, she felt a curious reluctance to dig further into his past.

There was something nauseating in listening to Miss Whitcham mouthing over his past loves, and Marisa could not help wondering how the garrulous old gossip had managed to survive in her present position.

There was no doubt that Miss Whitcham chattered familiarly with the servants, and what was more she hoarded in her mind every morsel of indiscretion.

"It is of course the obvious outlet for the frustration of an old maid!" Marisa told herself.

But she could not help wondering if one day she would be the same.

Her plans for the future would result in her living vicariously on other people's love affairs rather than having any of her own.

Then she thought she was merely depressed because the Duke, having returned home, had made it quite clear that he did not approve of the manner in which she was teaching Aline.

She had the inescapable feeling that sooner or later he would prevent her doing all she wished to do for the child and might even dismiss her.

There was a hard ruthlessness about the Duke which

she knew meant he would not scruple to remove anyone who stood in his path or opposed him too obviously.

"I do not want to leave yet," Marisa said aloud.

She knew that she would miss almost unbearably the pleasure she derived from the Library, the joy of riding the Duke's first-class horses and being surrounded with so much beauty and so many treasures.

If she was honest, it was more than that! She had, despite every resolution to the contrary, grown fond of Aline.

The child mattered to her more than she cared to admit. It had been like watching a plant grow, to see how Aline could blossom and develop under the right tuition.

"Are we never going to do any lessons?" Aline had asked after Marisa had been at the Castle for over a week.

Marisa smiled.

"You had a long history lesson this morning," she replied, "when we were talking about that magnificent picture of the Duke of Wellington which we found in the Blue Salon."

She paused to let her meaning sink in, then continued.

"Then, if you remember, we looked up the map of Belgium in the Library and saw where the Battle of Waterloo took place. We found a picture of it and also a sketch of the ball that was given at Brussels, the night before Napoleon advanced. That was a history and a geography lesson together."

"It was?" Aline asked increduously. "But that was not a proper lesson. I enjoyed it!"

"I hope you will always enjoy lessons I give," Marisa answered, "because I do not know how to teach you any other way."

"Oh, how wonderful! Wonderful!" Aline cried, and flinging her arms round Marisa's waist pressed herself close against her.

"It is such fun being with you," she said and Marisa had felt a sudden lump in her throat.

Yes, she had no wish to leave Vox Castle yet, and although she hated the Duke she loved his possessions.

"Tell me who else will be in the house-party?" she asked Miss Whitcham in an effort to distract her from a recitation of the Duke's lady-loves.

"It is certainly unnecessary for me to tell you that Lord and Lady Brooke are included," Miss Whitcham said with a smile. "The Prince will go nowhere unless Lady Brooke is one of the guests. They say he has never been so much in love as he is at the moment."

"It seems extraordinary," Marisa remarked, "considering His Royal Highness must be fifty this year."

"And Lady Brooke is thirty-one. But what has age to do with it?" Miss Whitcham enquired. "Of course, apart from the fact that His Royal Highness is extremely attractive to women, Lady Brooke enjoys all the comforts of moving in Royal circles."

She smiled knowingly and went on.

"I am told that during the racing season she travelled with the Prince in his special train, and of course she sits in the Royal Box. There are a great many advantages in being, if not His Royal Highness's wife, the Queen of his heart."

"Is it to be a big party?" Marisa asked.

"We will be fourteen this evening," Miss Whitcham replied. "I have the names all set out here. Tomorrow we will be twenty for luncheon, thirty for dinner and about the same on Sunday."

"What a lot of arranging you have to do," Marisa exclaimed.

"I take it in my stride," Miss Whitcham boasted. "I have done it for so many years. Of course the Prince's visit is different from other people's. For one thing we have to have a Post Office installed in the house and usually a whole wing in the staff quarters is set aside for his entourage."

"Does he bring many servants with him?" Marisa enquired.

"Two valets," Miss Whitcham answered, "his own footman who wears the Royal livery and stands behind his chair at meal-times and serves him. Two loaders if he is shooting, a Gentleman-in-Waiting and one or two Equerries. If the Princess accompanies His Royal Highness, the numbers rise to about twenty-five."

"Good heavens, it is quite an army!"

"The Prince is Heir to the Throne, my dear," Miss Whitcham said.

Marisa had already been told that Lord and Lady Wantage would be among the guests and she had hoped that she could keep the information from Aline.

But unfortunately Miss Whitcham came into the School-Room the following morning while Marisa and Aline were having breakfast.

"I forgot to tell you, Miss Mitton," she said, "that usually when there is a party, Aline goes down to the Drawing-Room at five o'clock while they are having tea. You will accompany her of course and wait discreetly at the back of the room until it is time to bring her upstairs again."

"Could I not leave her there?" Marisa asked quickly.

"No, of course not!" Miss Whitcham said in a shocked tone. "A governess always waits."

Miss Whitcham turned to leave the room and then in a scolding voice which Marisa thought altogether unnecessary, she said to Aline:

"Lady Wantage will be here, Aline, and I hope if she asks after that beautiful doll she gave you, you will not tell her how wantonly you smashed it to pieces. It would, I am quite sure, hurt Her Ladyship to know that her gesture of kindness was treated in such a disgraceful manner."

Aline put down her knife and fork, and the frown which had so often distorted her face made her eyebrows almost meet across her small nose.

"I will tell her the truth," she said rudely. "I will tell her what I have done with that stupid old doll. I am too old for dolls—Miss Mitton said so."

"That is quite enough, Aline," Marisa said in a quiet voice, "we will discuss it later when we are—alone."

She looked at Miss Whitcham as she spoke and the older woman could not but take the hint.

"You had better behave yourself," she said as a parting shot at Aline, "or your father will have something to say about it."

As she went from the room, Aline jumped up from the table.

"I hate Lady Wantage!" she said. "I do not want her presents! If she brings me any more I will throw them at her."

Marisa had learnt of old that it was no good arguing with Aline when she was in that sort of mood.

"If we do not hurry," she said also rising from the table, "we will keep the horses waiting. I have planned for us to take a long ride today. So hurry and get your boots on."

She went from the room before Aline could say anything more, and then when they were both ready she hurried the little girl downstairs and out through a side door towards the stables.

Aline was sulking and still scowling, but Marisa ignored it.

She knew that exercise and fresh air were the best possible antidote for bad temper and sure enough, after they had galloped for over quarter of an hour, Aline was smiling again.

They rode in a different direction from any that they had taken before, for Marisa had made up her mind to keep Aline away from the house for the whole morning.

She had hoped that she would have had a chance later in the day to break the fact that Lord and Lady Wantage were to be among her father's guests.

But now that Miss Whitcham had let the cat out of the bag she could only hope that if the child were sufficiently tired and relaxed, she would not feel so aggressive.

They had ridden for over an hour and the land was becoming progressively more hilly, until quite unexpectantly they came upon an ugly sight.

The hillside had suffered excaration and there were great mounds of slag, rusting machinery, a crumbling kiln and open holes propped up with sleepers of wood.

"What on earth is that?" Marisa asked in surprise.

It seemed incongruous amongst the green beauty of the woods which were so much a part of the rest of the Estate.

"That's the old iron mine," Aline answered.

"How interesting!" Marisa exclaimed. "I know there used to be lots of small iron mines in Sussex at the beginning of the century, but I have never seen one and I thought they were all worked out."

"So is this one," Aline said. "They've moved now to another site not far away. I heard Miss Whitcham and

Nanny saying how rough and vulgar the men are who work in the mine. I am not supposed to ride this way."

"Why did you not tell me so?" Marisa asked. "Although I can see no harm in your doing so."

"Nor can I," Aline said, "it is only Nanny being an old fusspot. And you know how Miss Whitcham thinks everyone is vulgar who is not a friend of the Prince of Wales."

Marisa laughed, she could not help it.

"The world is full of snobs, Aline. While we are here, let us look at the new mine."

They trotted on for about a mile, and then riding over the top of a low incline, they saw lying beneath them trucks filled with lumps of iron ore standing outside dark apertures in the hillside.

There was a large heap of slag and another of charcoal near what appeared to be a very primitive kiln.

There were a number of men standing or sitting amongst the debris, they did not seem to be working.

About a quarter of a mile away there was a small hamlet. The houses looked poor and dilapidated. Some of them were nothing better than huts, the roofs were patched, and most of the windows lacked glass.

"Does this belong to your father?" she asked Aline.

"Of course," Aline answered. "He owns everything for miles and miles and miles."

"It does not look a very attractive place," Marisa said almost to herself.

"Nanny says that people like that are little better than animals."

"But they are still people," Marisa said gently. "They have children who have to be fed, children whom they love, children who cry if they are unhappy and who have very few toys and luxuries such as you have, Aline. I think we have found where we can send your toys."

"You said I could give them myself," Aline said.

Marisa hesitated.

"I will have to ask if that will be possible," she said. "Perhaps your father will not allow you to go to the mining village."

"I want to give my dolls to a poor little girl," Aline replied, "I want to see if she's pleased."

"We will have to think about it," Marisa replied.

She was just going to turn away when three of the men came up the hill. When they saw Marisa and Aline on their horses, they stared at them with undisguised curiosity.

They were rough types, smoking short clay pipes, caps on the back of their untidy heads and handkerchiefs round their necks.

They passed quite close to the horses and Marisa, who had always lived in the country and knew one was expected to greet those whom one met casually, said:

"Good morning."

The men seemed surprised that she should address them, and then one of them, an older man, pulled his forelock in a respectful manner and replied:

" 'morning, Lady. Nice day!"

"Yes it is," Marisa answered.

A younger man was staring at Aline.

"Be this th' Dook's little gal?"

"My Papa is the Duke," Aline answered before Marisa could speak.

"Oi thinks so," the man remarked in a smiling fashion and spat!

The men walked on, Marisa turned her horse to ride back towards the valley.

When she reached the flat ground she looked back and saw that the men silhouetted against the sky were standing watching them.

"They look rough because they have to work in dirty surroundings," she said to Aline, thinking it was wise to drive home a lesson. "Whether they are mining iron, coal or slate, the dust and dirt gets into the miners' nose, hair and eyes. Iron is one of the oldest metals in the world, and an iron blade probably 5000 years old was found in one of the pyramids in Egypt."

She continued telling Aline about the iron bars used in very primitive times by the Early Britains as currency and how the magnificent gates at Vox were of wrought iron.

Aline was interested, as she always was, when Marisa gave her information in the form of a story.

They arrived back at the Castle just in time for luncheon.

When the meal was finished Aline lay down for an hour and Marisa went to her own room.

She was sitting reading a book enjoying every word of it, when she heard a carriage drive up to the front door.

Curiosity made her rise and she saw, to her surprise, a lady dressed in the height of fashion descend from a brougham drawn by two horses.

It seemed unlikely for a member of the house-party to be arriving so early, because, as Marisa well knew, it was usual for the guests to assemble between five and six.

This allowed the servants time to unpack before dinner and did not embarrass the host and hostess by having several extra hours to fill in before a party properly began.

There was however nothing to be gained by speculation as to who the newcomer might be, and so Marisa had seated herself again in her chair, when Miss Whitcham came into the room.

"Am I disturbing you, Miss Mitton?" she enquired.

Marisa knew by the look on her face that she was longing to talk to someone.

She had grown accustomed in the last few weeks to have Miss Whitcham confiding in her whenever a crisis occurred.

Miss Whitcham obviously found her a more intelligent companion than Nanny, and she was the only person in the house with whom Miss Whitcham felt herself to be on equal terms.

"What has happened?" Marisa asked, knowing it must be something sensational for Miss Whitcham to climb the stairs to her room.

"You will not believe what has happened, Miss Mitton," was the answer, "but Lady Wantage has arrived alone!"

"Alone?" Marisa questioned.

"Yes indeed. And I am informed that Lord Wantage will not arrive until tomorrow. It surprises me, it does really."

"Why?" Marisa asked.

"I have heard, through channels that I will not mention," Miss Whitcham said lowering her voice, "that Lord Wantage had been rather difficult about His Grace when

they were staying in Scotland. So why should he now deliberately throw them together?"

Marisa did not press Miss Whitcham as to where she
had obtained such information. She knew only too well
one of the Duke's valets was under her thumb.

"Will that not throw out your dinner-table?" she
enquired.

"Of course it will," Miss Whitcham replied. "But His
Grace tells me that fortunately Lord Frederick Farrington
is staying only ten miles away. We have sent a groom
post-haste to ask him to dine and stay the night."

"You do not wish to be thirteen?" Marisa asked with a
smile.

"I should think not indeed!" Miss Whitcham said almost with a cry. "The Prince will never, under any circumstances, sit down with such an unlucky number at the
table. His Royal Highness is very superstitious."

"Is he?" Marisa enquired. "It seems so childish somehow."

"I always give orders when the Prince is here that the
mattresses should not be turned on Friday, and the pantry
staff are very particular to see that the knives are not
crossed on the table."

Marisa laughed.

"I am speaking seriously," Miss Whitcham affirmed,
"the Prince is very particular about such things. I am told
that once when a dinner was given in his honour and the
fourteenth guest was late, he refused to leave the
Drawing-room."

Marisa laughed again.

"I would rather have my job than yours!"

"So would I at the moment," Miss Whitcham replied.
"But can you imagine Lady Wantage being so blatant as
to arrive three hours before she is expected. Of course everyone in the Castle is talking, and if the rest of the guests
find out there will be a lot of raised eyebrows, I can assure you."

"Does His Grace know she is here?" Marisa enquired.

"Fortunately he had not gone out," Miss Whitcham replied. "He was in his Study. I expect that as soon as the
door was closed, he welcomed her with open arms and
they will have a nice cosy time together—alone."

Miss Whitcham seemed to smack her lips at the prospect before she said:

"But I cannot stay here talking to you! I have so much to do."

She paused at the doorway and there was a smirk on her face as she added:

"I must see that everything is right for Her Ladyship in the suite exactly opposite that of His Grace."

She closed the door behind her and Marisa sat back in her chair.

This was just the sort of thing that she had wanted to discover before she came to Vox. She should be scribbling it down on the manuscript which lay in the locked leather bag in her wardrobe.

"I cannot do it now," she excused herself, "it is time to take Aline for a walk."

She went into the School-room, looked out of the window and saw it had begun to rain. Aline came from the bed-room rubbing her eyes.

"I have been asleep."

"That is what I expected," Marisa smiled. "We rode a long way this morning."

"Are we going for a walk?"

"It is raining," Marisa replied. "I wondered if instead you would like to have a music lesson?"

The familiar scowl appeared on Aline's forehead.

"I hate music!"

"What a pity," Marisa replied, "I enjoy it."

She crossed to the piano as she spoke, opened it and sat down on the stool.

There had been so many other things to do since she had arrived that she had not, until now, suggested that Aline should learn to play.

She had however seen some stereotyped pieces on top of the piano and guessed the previous governesses had made the child practise innumerable scales.

She had always privately thought to herself it was enough to make anyone dislike music.

Now she sat down at the piano and started to play the popular song which, sung by Hayden Coffin, had swept like wild fire into every Victorian Drawing-room and was sung or whistled by every errand-boy.

> Then why should we wait 'til tomorrow?
> You're Queen of my heart tonight.

Marisa sang in a soft melodious voice, and she knew without turning round that Aline had come a little nearer to the piano.

She went straight into "Monkey on a Stick" which Lettie Lynn had made such a success and then she started to sing the song from *Carmen Up-to-Date* which was a smash hit at the Gaiety.

> Hush, Hush, here comes the Bogey Man,
> So hide your heads beneath the clothes
>   —he'll take you if he can.

She sang it right through, then she said to Aline:
"Sing it with me."

She played the chorus over twice and Aline, shyly at first and then her voice getting firmer and louder, joined in.

Marisa took her hands off the piano keys and turned round to face her.

"Do you not think that is fun?" she asked.

"That's not a music lesson," Aline said suspiciously.

"Why not?" Marisa answered. "Let me look at your hands."

Aline held them out palm outwards, for Marisa's inspection. She stared at them for a moment, a surprised look on her face and then she said:

"You have very pretty hands, Aline, and with that wide stretch between your thumb and your first finger, you can easily reach an octave. Try to pick out the tune with me. It is not difficult."

Marisa had been right: Aline had quite an accurate ear and in a little while she managed to play the theme with one finger on the treble keys while Marisa vamped in the base.

"I like that!" Aline cried triumphantly when they had played the whole chorus without a mistake. "Teach me some more!"

"Of course I will," Marisa replied. "We will ask Miss

Whitcham if we can have all the new songs from London and we will play and sing them."

"I need not do exercises?" Aline asked.

"Not unless you want to get your fingers supple," Marisa answered. "Sometimes they can be rather fun, like this."

She played a trill up and down the keyboard.

"Oh I would like to do that," Aline cried.

"Well, try," Marisa suggested.

The child was trying to copy her when there came a knock at the door.

"Who is it?" Marisa enquired.

The door was opened and a footman stood there.

"His Grace's compliments, Miss, will you bring Miss Aline down to the Blue Salon?"

Marisa looked at the clock. The hands pointed to five minutes past four.

"Very good, James," she replied.

She wondered why Aline was required so early and thought somewhat apprehensively that Lady Wantage might have brought her another present.

"I wonder why she is so attentive to the child?" she asked herself.

Then her lips curled at the thought that it was an old trick to make up to a widower through his motherless child.

She looked at Aline and realised that she had been dressed to go walking.

It only took a few minutes to change her sensible cotton frock for an elaborate creation of frills, lace and a wide pink sash.

"I hate this dress," Aline announced.

"So do I," Marisa agreed, "it is much too young for you. When this party is over, Aline, we will go to the nearest town and see if we can find you something nicer."

"Can we really?" Aline enquired, her eyes lighting up.

"But if you are to wear older dresses, you will have to behave in an older manner," Marisa admonished. "Older people do not make scenes, and if Lady Wantage gives you a present you must accept it gracefully. Just thank her politely."

Marisa paused and then went on:

"And if she asks after the doll she gave you, just say it is comfortable. After all we have made it comfortable, have we not, in the sand-pit?"

Aline laughed.

"You promise," Marisa said.

"I promise . . . that is what I will say," Aline answered.

"You are ready now," Marisa said, "I will just tidy my own hair."

She hurried from the School-room into her own bedroom.

Not expecting to have to go down-stairs without changing, she was wearing an expensively simple dress of pale mauve cambric ornamented with mauve ribbon. It made her look very young and accentuated the golden glints in her hair.

"I ought to change," Marisa told herself thinking of her gown with the puritan cuffs and collar which was far more suitable for a governess.

But there was no time, the Duke would be waiting, and if they delayed it might make him annoyed with Aline.

She hurried back into the School-room. Aline was waiting and holding in her hand a little silk bag which matched the pink of her sash.

"Do you want to take that with you?" Marisa asked.

"I've put my handkerchief in it," Aline said.

"It was sensible of you to remember," Marisa said approvingly.

She took Aline by the hand and they hurried down the stairs. When they reached the Grand Staircase it seemed to Marisa that Aline was moving slower.

"You promised me, Aline," she said.

"I will keep my promise," Aline answered.

"And you will thank Lady Wantage nicely if she has brought a present for you?"

They crossed the Hall and one of the footmen opened the door into the Blue Salon. The Duke and Lady Wantage were seated side by side on a sofa in front of the fire.

It struck Marisa as she entered that the Duke's expression was stern and as if he was not particularly amused, but Her Ladyship was soft and seductive.

She was looking, Marisa had to admit, extremely attractive in an elaborate tea-gown into which she had changed on her arrival.

Of pale blue chiffon it accentuated her tiny waist, frothed round her feet and matched the vivid blue of her pretty but empty eyes.

"Oh darling little Aline!" she gushed. "How I have been longing to see you! Come and tell me what you have been doing with your dear little self since I was last here."

Marisa gave Aline a push as she realised the child was making no effort to go forward.

Lady Wantage held out her arms in a gesture that was almost theatrical.

"Come to me, little one," she coaxed, "I know how lonely you must be here in this great big Castle all by yourself."

Slowly, each step seeming to take a long time, Aline advanced across the carpet towards Lady Wantage.

Then, when she had almost reached her, she looked at her father.

"I went riding this morning, Papa."

It seemed to Marisa watching there was not a flicker of interest in the Duke's expression.

"Did you?" he remarked indifferently.

Marisa felt she could strike him.

Could he not understand, after what she had told him, that he should not have ordered the child downstairs to meet Lady Wantage, and at least he might appear interested in her.

"We went for miles and miles," Aline said, "right out as far as the iron mine."

The Duke's head turned sharply towards Marisa.

"The iron mine!" he exclaimed. "There is no reason for Aline to go in that direction, Miss Mitton."

"I am sorry, Your Grace," Marisa answered, "I did not realise it was out of bounds until after we had been there. No-one had told me."

"I should have thought it was an unnecessarily long ride for a little girl of Aline's age."

There was so much reproof in his tone that Marisa felt her resentment over-coming her caution.

"You were hunting when you were nine, Your Grace."

"There is no comparison," the Duke snapped.

Lady Wantage had dropped her arms and was listening. Now she seemed to notice Marisa's appearance for the first time.

Her china-blue eyes grew hard as they saw the vivid red hair, the manner in which the mauve gown accentuated the lovely curves of Marisa's figure.

"I do not think I have met this young woman," she said. "Surely she cannot be Aline's new governess."

"This is Miss Mitton," the Duke said and Marisa dropped a small curtsey.

"I should have thought that she was too young for such a position," Lady Wantage said in a whisper that was perfectly audible to Marisa.

"She is not too young," Aline interrupted before the Duke could speak. "And she teaches me very well! I have learnt lots and lots of things since she has been here."

"That is good," Lady Wantage said without enthusiasm. "Look, Aline, I have brought you a present. Was that not clever of me to remember?"

She took a small parcel from a table beside the sofa.

"There it is, packed especially for you. I only hope the other people who are coming here tonight will remember you as I have done, and then you will have plenty of lovely presents to open."

She held out the small parcel to Aline who appeared reluctant to accept it.

"Take it and say thank you," the Duke said sharply.

"Thank you," Aline said obediently.

She took the parcel and set it down on a chair beside the Duke.

"Are you not going to open it?" Lady Wantage enquired and as Aline did not reply she added:

"I expect you are shy, you poor little thing. Open it when you get upstairs. I am sure you will want to show it to your lovely doll from Paris. Have you been having happy games with her?"

There was a silence. Marisa held her breath and then Aline said:

"She is—very—comfortable."

"Tucked up in bed!" Lady Wantage exclaimed. "Is that not sweet? Valerius, I find your daughter quite enchanting!"

She turned towards the Duke as she spoke, her blue eyes raised to his, an expression on her face which Marisa was sure she intended to look soft and maternal.

The Duke however was not looking at her.

"Now you have your present, Aline," he said, "you can go upstairs. If anyone else asks to see you, Miss Mitton will bring you down later."

"I am sure everyone will want to see your daughter, Valerius," Lady Wantage said with a little laugh, although there seemed to be no reason for laughter.

Aline was standing staring at Lady Wantage and Marisa felt instinctively she was concocting something.

"Come and kiss me good-bye, you sweet little thing," Lady Wantage said, "and then run upstairs and do as your Papa says. You must always do what your Papa wants, as we all do."

Again she gave a silly little laugh. Someone had once described it as a tinkling bell and she had never forgotten it.

Aline put her hand inside the little bag which dangled from her arm.

"I have a—present for—you," she said slowly.

"How very very sweet of you! I shall treasure it always," Lady Wantage said with a self-satisfied smile.

Aline drew out her hand and held it out tightly clenched to Lady Wantage.

Marisa wondered apprehensively what the gift could be. Then as Lady Wantage held out her white hands, Aline opened her fingers.

Something small and brown rested for a moment on Lady Wantage's palm, then sprang into her lap.

There was a shriek—a scream of sheer horror—before Lady Wantage was clinging to the Duke, crying hysterically:

"Take it . . . away! Take it . . . away! I cannot . . . bear it."

Marisa moved hurriedly across the room. Before she could reach Aline, the child had begun to laugh.

"Oh God . . . where is it . . . I cannot stand mice! Save me . . . Valerius."

The Duke disentangled himself from Lady Wantage's clinging arms.

"Go upstairs, Aline!" he thundered. "I am ashamed of you!"

Then he glanced at Marisa as she bent to take Aline by the hand.

"If this is the result of your new-fangled type of education, Miss Mitton," he said icily, "it is not very successful."

Marisa hurried Aline from the room. Even when they had reached the top of the staircase they could still hear Lady Wantage's sobs and cries.

They were inside the school-room before Marisa spoke.

"Where could you have found a mouse?" she asked.

"In my bed-room," Aline answered. "Nanny set a trap because I told her there was one scratching in the wall. She does not like the traps that kill them, and so it was caught in a little cage. They are drowned afterwards in a bucket down-stairs."

"What am I to say to you, Aline?" Marisa asked. "You know it was naughty."

"She gave me a present and I gave her one," Aline answered.

There was silence and then Marisa asked:

"Did you know she was frightened of mice?"

"Yes," Aline replied. "Last time she was here I heard her lady's maid telling Nanny that she was terrified of them."

"Then it was particularly unkind of you," Marisa said sternly. "Everyone has something of which they are particularly afraid. You knew Miss Graves was frightened of snakes, you knew Lady Wantage was terrified of mice. What is your special fear, Aline?"

There was a long pause and then Aline said in a very small voice:

"You will ... not ... shut me up in a ... dark ... cupboard, Miss Mitton?"

"Why should I do that?" Marisa asked.

"Miss Thompson did. I screamed and screamed and Nanny said if she did it again she would send for the Doctor."

"Then if you remember how frightened you were in a dark cupboard," Marisa said, "you know how frightened other people can be."

"I would not frighten you, Miss Mitton," Aline said, "I love you."

"That is not the point," Marisa answered. "It is cruel to frighten anyone. And now what do you think your punishment ought to be?"

"Can I choose?" Aline asked.

"You can make a suggestion," Marisa replied. "It has to be a real punishment, no cheating."

"I suppose I would mind most if you didn't tell me any more stories," Aline said in a forlorn voice.

"Very well," Marisa said, "no stories for two days and I think too you should go to bed at once. Your Papa will certainly not want you down-stairs again this evening."

"Do you think he's very angry with me?" Aline enquired.

"Not only with you," Marisa answered, "but also with me. You have made it difficult in future, Aline, to do all the amusing things we have been doing together because now he will not approve of my methods."

"Do you mean he'll stop me ... shooting, riding without a ... leading-rein and looking up ... secrets in the ... Library?" Aline enquired.

"He may do so," Marisa answered.

"Oh, Miss Mitton, I'm sorry! I didn't mean to make Papa angry. It's only that I knew Lady Wantage would scream and cry if she saw a mouse, and that it would make him see how silly she is. She only makes a fuss of me because she wants to show off to Papa. She doesn't really like me."

Marisa smiled to herself. It was obviously difficult for anyone to deceive a child as bright as Aline.

She too had felt that Lady Wantage was showing off merely to impress the Duke, but of course she could not say so.

"Forgive me, please forgive me, Miss Mitton," Aline pleaded.

For the first time since Marisa had known her, there were tears of contrition in her eyes rather than tears of anger.

Impulsively she knelt down on the floor and put her arms round the small body.

"Do not cry, darling," she said. "It was very naughty,

as you know, but somehow we must try and make your father forgive you."

Aline threw her arms round Marisa's neck.

"I love you, Miss Mitton," she said. "Promise you'll not go away and leave me because I'm naughty?"

"I will not go away because you are naughty," Marisa said. "If ever I go away, it will not be for that reason."

"You . . . promise?" Aline asked.

"I promise," Marisa answered.

She held the child tightly in her arms and as she did so she knew that without meaning to, against all her resolutions when she had come to the Castle, she had grown to love Aline.

To love her as she had never loved a child before.

Chapter Five

Marisa was brushing her long hair which fell below her waist, when there came a sharp knock at the door. Without waiting for an answer, Miss Whitcham burst into the bed-room.

"Quick, Miss Mitton!" she exclaimed. "You are to dine with the house-party."

"With the house-party?" Marisa repeated in astonishment.

"Yes—yes," Miss Whitcham replied, breathless from having run upstairs. "Lady Elcho has arrived with a temperature and gone straight to bed! That leaves thirteen for dinner."

Marisa smiled.

She realised her momentary importance. She could refuse to acquiesce in being called in at the last moment and this would leave the Duke in an uncomfortable predicament.

"There is not time to get anyone else," Miss Witcham explained, "and it was His Grace who thought of you. He said, 'Tell Miss Mitton to come down to dinner. I suppose she has an evening-dress?' "

The words made Marisa seethe with anger.

How dare the Duke speak about her as if she was such a nobody that she had never been to a dinner-party? How dare he treat her as a servant who could be commanded to do this or do that without even saying please!

"I will refuse!" she first decided. "I will say that I have a headache and have retired to bed."

Then her anger made her change her mind.

She would show the Duke that indeed she had an evening-dress. She would show him that she knew how to behave even in such company as included the Prince of Wales.

He might think he was ordering downstairs a subservient little governess, but he would find he was mistaken!

"Very well, Miss Whitcham," she said, "I will dine downstairs as His Grace suggests."

"You will have to hurry," Miss Whitcham said nervously. "It is already twenty past seven."

"I will be in time," Marisa answered, "but send me one of the more experienced housemaids. I will need help with my gown."

"I will do that," Miss Whitcham replied. "I must rush and arrange the seating at the dinner table for the third time!"

She bustled from the room and Marisa rose from the stool on which she had been seated and walked to the wardrobe.

She pulled open the door and with a little smile on her lips contemplated the evening-gowns which had been included amongst the clothes given her by her aunt.

Lady Berrington had always been wildly extravagant, and her maid must have taken her literally when she told her to pack everything that was coloured for Marisa.

There was no less than seven evening-gowns, each more elaborate and more expensive than the last, most of them unworn.

Marisa looked at them for a moment and then returned to the dressing-table.

She twisted her long red hair, piling it high and elegantly on her head in the style set by Princess Alexandra. Then she went to her leather bag which was always kept locked.

On top of the manuscript was a box containing the jewellery which had belonged to her grandmother.

"My mother left it for my eldest son," the Earl had explained when he gave it to Marisa, "but as I have no son, I would rather you wore it than George's frivolous, flirtatious wife."

He had always spoken scathingly about his sister-in-law because he disliked Kitty Berrington.

Marisa knew it would be useless to tell him that her

Uncle George was entitled to the family heirlooms and indeed she had been glad to have the jewellery herself.

Not only was it a beautiful possession, but at the back of her mind she could not help realising that it would always be an insurance against poverty.

Now she drew from the velvet-lined case three diamond stars. She knew that, because the Prince of Wales was present, every woman would be wearing a tiara or huge diamond pins in her hair.

Marisa set the largest diamond star high over her forehead. The other two on either side. Then she clasped round her neck a diamond necklace.

It was not exceptionally valuable, but it was of exquisite workmanship, and the sparkle of the gems seemed to match the light of battle in her eyes.

Finally as a housemaid came hurrying into the room, Marisa turned to the wardrobe.

She had already decided which gown to wear. It was one she had thought was far too elaborate and grand for her ever to have an excuse for wearing it.

Of green tulle it was spangled all over with tiny diamante. The train was a froth of tulle frills which were echoed by the clouds which framed her white shoulders.

The décolletage was slightly daring for an unmarried girl, but Marisa did not care.

She was ready to do battle with the Duke and she knew, when finally she looked in the mirror, that she appeared undeniably lovely.

It would be difficult for the Duke to recognise the crushed little governess whom he had berated for his daughter's misdemeanours.

There was nothing meek and subservient about Marisa as she moved slowly down the Grand Staircase.

With her head held high, her long neck encircled by the diamonds and the vivid green of her dress making her skin appear white as a magnolia, she was both outstanding and beautiful.

She timed her entrance into the Drawing-room where the guests were assembled at exactly two minutes to eight.

The Butler took one startled glance at her as she reached the Hall, and opening the door announced:

"Miss Mitton, Your Grace."

It seemed to Marisa there was a silence as she advanced across the Aubusson carpet to where the dinner party had assembled in front of the fireplace.

For a moment it was difficult to recognise a familiar face, then the Duke detached himself from the others and came towards her.

"I must thank you, Miss Mitton," he said, "for helping us avoid a very real crisis!"

He spoke conventionally, but Marisa with a feeling of triumph saw the surprise in his eyes as they flickered over the shining crown she had made of her hair and the fashionable elegance of her gown.

The Duke led her towards the Prince of Wales.

"May I present Miss Mitton, Sir?" he asked, "who has most kindly relieved us of the anxiety of being the unfortunate number of thirteen at dinner tonight."

Marisa sank in a deep curtsey.

"We are in your debt, Miss Mitton," the Prince said genially.

Then as Marisa rose he added with a twinkle in his eyes:

"Are you a very stern disciplinarian, Miss Mitton, because you certainly do not look it."

"No indeed, Sir," Marisa replied. "I follow your Royal Highness's example in foreign affairs by trying with persuasion and charm."

The Prince threw back his head and laughed, obviously delighted at the compliment. The Duke drew Marisa away to introduce her to the other ladies and gentlemen present.

They were just a sea of faces and Marisa found it difficult to think clearly and to remember their names until she found herself at dinner seated next to Mr. Arthur Balfour.

She recognised him from his photographs and she knew he had just been made the new Leader of the House of Commons.

She tried to remember all the things she had heard about him. Her father, despite his opposition to Mr. Balfour's politics, had spoken of his wit, and she remembered Mrs. Featherstone-Haugh saying: "He has a cool grace and a lovely bend of his head."

Then she recalled that Mrs. Featherstone-Haugh, continuing the conversation, had told her father that Mr. Balfour was deeply enamoured with the Viscountess Elcho.

That would account, Marisa realised, for Lady Elcho's inclusion in the house-party.

It was Her Ladyship's place she was taking at the dinner table and she supposed that if Mr. Balfour must be very disappointed at having to put up with her as a substitute for the woman he loved.

Mrs. Featherstone-Haugh had known Lady Elcho since she was a girl.

"Arthur Balfour fascinates her," Marisa could hear her telling her father. "She looks up to him in wonder and worship! And who can blame her? He is erudite, musical, has social distinction and a first class brain."

Mrs. Featherstone-Haugh had fluttered her eyelashes at her host and added:

"Besides all this Arthur Balfour can charm the birds off the trees, or any woman he fancies into his arms!"

"Just the vulgarity one would expect in a depraved society!" the Earl of Berrington had growled.

"Nonsense, Lionel!" Mrs. Featherstone-Haugh retorted. "Arthur Balfour could never be vulgar! He is a great gentleman and his love affairs are on a grand scale."

"Balzac said—'Great love affairs start with champagne and end with tisane'," the Earl quoted. "In England they end with a yawn and croquet!"

Marisa could still hear Mrs. Featherstone-Haugh's laughter. She was the only person who could entice her father out of his depressed moody attitude to life.

Now Marisa looked with interest and some curiosity at Mr. Balfour, at his broad clever brow and rather indolent eyes.

"Do you enjoy teaching?" he asked when they had been served with the first course.

The table was decorated with magnificent gold plate, enormous gold candelabra and ornamented with a profusion of purple orchids.

"I enjoy it very much," Marisa answered, "because I think if one teaches, one also learns."

She thought as she spoke about how much she had learnt about Aline and how to handle her since she had come to Vox Castle.

"You are right," Mr. Balfour said, "and an omnivorous, universal, insatiable curiosity about everything that can be known, is a pleasure that lasts longer than any other."

"I am sure that is true," Marisa smiled, "and certainly it is easy to find a great deal of pleasure here in the Castle where there is the most magnificent Library I have ever seen."

"And I believe our host keeps it up to date," Mr. Balfour said. "Do not omit, Miss Mitton, to teach his daughter to speak foreign languages as well as her father."

Marisa looked so surprised that Mr. Balfour said:

"You did not know what a good linguist the Duke is? I assure you he is exceptional. It has often been very advantageous to the Government."

"In what way?" Marisa asked curiously.

"The Prime Minister and the Foreign Secretary could answer that better than I can," Mr. Balfour replied. "But I am betraying no secrets when I tell you that the Duke is a very welcome guest on the many journeys His Royal Highness makes abroad, not only because of his company, but because of his fluency in the language of the country being visited."

"I had no idea," Marisa murmured almost beneath her breath.

It had astonished her that the Duke should be spoken of with such warmth by a man who was acknowledged to be outstandingly brilliant in the political world.

Seeing her surprise, Mr. Balfour looked amused.

"Could it be possible, Miss Mitton, that you are prepared to judge a man entirely superficially?"

"I had imagined I was more perceptive," Marisa replied, "but perhaps where the Duke is concerned I have a blind spot."

"It may be because he is your employer that you are afraid of him," Mr. Balfour suggested. "But having known the Duke for many years, I can assure you that what one perceives on the surface, is not important. Dig deep and you will find a man who, if he chose, could be of vital service to his country and a very real power in the House of Lords."

Mr. Balfour's attention was claimed by the lady on his

other side, and Marisa, feeling almost bemused by her astonishment at this new aspect of the Duke's character, turned to the gentleman on her left.

She remembered as she did so that he had been introduced to her as Lord Frederick Farrington and realised that he was the guest who had been sent for in such a hurry when Lord Wantage had defected at the last moment.

Lord Frederick was a fleshy red-faced man of about forty, with a fruity voice, bold protruding eyes and a thick sensuous mouth.

He was the type, Marisa thought, that she had expected to find in the fast set which surrounded the Prince of Wales.

As she turned towards him she felt, to her surprise, his knee against hers.

She thought it was an accident and moved aside, only to realise it had been intentional.

"You are far too fascinating to be a governess!" Lord Frederick said. "Where did Milverley find you? He must be more of a deep 'un than I imagined."

"I was recommended to my present position by Lady Berrington," Marisa said in a cold voice. "I was engaged in the Duke's absence by his secretary who runs the household."

"Kitty Berrington recommended you did she?" Lord Frederick chuckled. "Then I'll bet, having seen you, she wanted to be rid of you! Didn't want anything as pretty as you about when George was home!"

There was a familiarity about Lord Frederick's remarks which irritated Marisa.

But she realised there was no point in being rude, so she merely concentrated on her food, conscious all the time that his knee was trying to press hers.

"What is your history?" Lord Frederick asked in her ear. "I cannot believe that red hair like yours does not denote a fiery and passionate temperament! Or are you a Sleeping Beauty?"

"I have no answer for your questions," Marisa replied. "Can you not talk of something other than myself, a subject which I find exceptionally boring."

"Well I find you extremely interesting," Lord Frederick

retorted quite unabashed. "You are a beauty and it tempts me into wild indiscretions."

"Not at a party like this I hope," Marisa said in what she hoped was a warning tone.

"We shall not be here all night," Lord Frederick said with an unconcealed innuendo in his voice.

Marisa found her dislike of the man increasing with every word he spoke.

He was behaving just as she expected gentlemen in the social world would behave towards a woman who was unprotected by a husband and in a position where it would be difficult for her to defend herself.

"Are you shooting tomorrow, Lord Frederick?" she asked in a manner which she thought would show him quite clearly she was not prepared to go on listening to his insinuations.

"You are adorable," he replied. "You delight me when you pretend to be severe. Your lips were made to kiss, my dear, not to scold."

Infuriated, Marisa turned away from him towards Mr. Balfour, only to find the Statesman was deep in conversation with the lady on his other side.

Marisa knew that unless she wished to upset the whole table, she must continue to talk with Lord Frederick.

He saw her predicament and laughed.

"There is nothing you can do about it," he mocked, "so make the best of me, my pretty little Temptress, and tell me about yourself."

"There is nothing to tell," Marisa answered. "As you know already I am Aline's governess and I am invited here tonight only because otherwise there would have been thirteen at the table."

"You are the lucky fourteenth and I am lucky to be sitting next to you," Lord Frederick said. "Shall I tell you you have the whitest skin of any woman I have ever seen and your reproving green eyes are belied by your red mouth? I am prepared, my enchanting little teacher, to fall madly in love with you."

"I wish you would talk to me sensibly," Marisa pleaded. "Are you not interested in politics, art, music, racing, anything rather than this aimless and futile flirtation?"

"Even Cinderella was permitted to captivate Prince Charming," Lord Frederick remarked. "And as His Royal Highness is otherwise engaged, I must attempt to deputise for him!"

Marisa smiled scornfully.

"Like Cinderella, I too vanish at midnight. So instead of making me angry, please make the time we must spend in each other's company, pass pleasantly."

"Nothing could be more enjoyable as far as I am concerned," Lord Frederick answered, "and do not forget: Cinderella was finally run to earth."

"Only because she left her glass slipper behind," Marisa replied almost tartly. "I assure you I will keep both mine firmly on my feet."

"We will see," Lord Frederick remarked and once again Marisa could feel his knee seeking hers.

Every time she was forced to speak to him he continued to pay her compliments. It was not so much what he said, but the way he looked at her which made Marisa want to shudder.

There was something oily and unpleasant about him and she was sure he was like the great majority of the gentlemen of leisure who had little to occupy their minds.

Pursuing a woman was just another sport. They went after any female who attracted their attention and were relentless in their hunt, satisfied only when the woman's surrender was complete and the excitement over.

Marisa looked round the table thinking how easily she could lampoon the party.

There was no mistaking the light in the Prince's eyes as he spoke to Lady Brooke who sat on his right, there was no pretence about the manner in which Lady Wantage was fawning upon the Duke.

She had looked at Marisa with active dislike as the Duke had introduced her before dinner to the other guests.

And Marisa had known that Lady Wantage's cold blue eyes had taken in every detail of the expensive gown she wore, the diamonds round her neck and the stars glistening in her red hair.

She would not miss the opportunity, Marisa was sure, of being unpleasant.

Sure enough, as soon as the ladies had withdrawn to the Drawing-room, Lady Wantage, in a voice which was meant to be heard by all the other women, remarked:

"I am admiring your diamonds, Miss Mitton, and you will forgive me if I am a little curious as to where you could have obtained them."

As Lady Wantage spoke Marisa suddenly realised what she and perhaps the other ladies present were thinking.

It had never crossed her mind that to appear dressed in a gown which must have cost far more than a governess's salary for the whole year and glittering with diamonds, was for someone in her position, to suggest that she was the recipient of such gifts from the Duke.

Could anyone really credit that any gentleman worthy of the name would be prepared to pass off his mistress as the governess of his child?

But she knew, as she looked into Lady Wantage's suspicious face and realised that the other ladies were listening for her reply, that that was exactly what they did think.

"My diamonds were left me by my grandmother," Marisa said truthfully. "This is the first time I have worn them and I am very grateful they can make their debut on such a memorable occasion."

The ladies listening almost heaved a sigh of relief and then Lady Wantage, her words sounding as if they had been dipped in poison, continued.

"And your dress? That very expensive and elegant gown, Miss Mitton, was that also a gift from your grandmother?"

It was with difficulty that Marisa did not reply that Lady Wantage should mind her own business.

Instead, gently, in a voice which merely sounded sincere, she answered:

"My gown was a gift from a woman friend who has unexpectedly to wear mourning for a year. She gave me a large number of dresses, but again I did not expect to have the opportunity of wearing anything so elaborate."

Almost like magic Marisa saw the suspicion vanish from the expressions of those listening, and then Lady Brooke with the charm which was famous crossed the hearth and sat down beside her.

"Tell me how you enjoy being at Vox, Miss Mitton," she said beguilingly. "It has always been one of my favourite houses."

Marisa succumbed immediately to the fascination of the lovely eyes which seemed to twinkle with laughter and yet held an unusual compassion and understanding.

They talked for a little while and then Marisa said:

"Shall I play the piano?"

She felt it would excuse Lady Brooke from feeling that she should talk with her further when she would obviously prefer to be conversing with her friends.

She was well aware of the kindness the more experienced woman was showing her in singling her out for such attention after Lady Wantage's rudeness.

"I think that would be very nice," Lady Brooke replied. "Although you must not be offended if no-one listens."

"I only intended it to be a soft background for their conversation," Marisa said with a little smile and Lady Brooke smiled at her in response as she rose from the sofa and walked to the piano.

It was the finest instrument on which she had ever played, and soon she forgot where she was as her fingers sped over the keys in one of Chopin's waltzes.

She was almost surprised to find the gentlemen had joined the ladies and they were all talking in front of the fire.

She wondered if she should stop playing and rise to her feet as the Prince was there, but then decided it would only be an embarrassment to stand on the edge of a circle when all the other people knew each other well.

As she decided to go on playing, she saw the Duke's head turn towards her.

She could not tell at a distance whether he was approved or not of what she was doing, but she could not help thinking how outstanding he was even amongst his equals.

There was something about his broad shoulders, the carriage of his head, the clear-cut perfection of his features, which made him seem different.

She might dislike him, but she knew he was a man no-one could ignore.

In a way, she thought as she played, it was not surprising to learn he was different from the dilettante and waster that she had thought him to be.

She was well aware that Mr. Balfour could have said a great deal more had he wished to do so.

There was no reason for him to have praised the Duke unless he really was respected in political circles.

Marisa knew now why all the latest books from French authors were to be found in the Library. The same applied to those in German, Spanish and Italian.

The Librarian was an old man who came to the Library two days a week to keep the catalogue up to date and to place the latest volumes in their proper place on the shelves.

"I might have guessed they were the Duke's choice," Marisa told herself and wondered why she should have been so obstruse as to think the books had been the taste of the Librarian.

She longed to talk to the Duke about some of his latest acquisitions, and then she realised it was very unlikely they would ever have such a conversation.

As she thought of it, Marisa realised with almost a sinking of her heart that there was every likelihood of the Duke dismissing her on Monday. He would not over-look Aline's behaviour to Lady Wantage.

There would be explanations to be made, she would have to justify her attitude towards her recreant pupil and perhaps dissuade the Duke from punishing his daughter as severely as he might wish to do.

At the thought she felt her interest in the evening ebb away.

It had been exciting to come downstairs, to be at a dinner-party which included the Prince of Wales, to see the glittering jewels of the women guests who looked like lovely flowers.

They had graced a table which was magnificent beyond anything Marisa had ever anticipated.

The footmen with powdered hair behind every chair, the floral displays in the Hall and in the Salons, the food, superlative and delectable beyond her wildest imaginings, were all things she knew would be etched indelibly on her mind.

She had seen grandeur, she had seen elegance, she had

seen a luxury of which she knew her father would have violently disapproved. Yet, like a page of history, it was hers for all time, something she would never be able to forget.

She finished playing a piece and rested her fingers for a moment wondering what she should choose next.

Then suddenly she was conscious of the overwhelming smell of a rich cigar and heard behind her the odious voice of Lord Frederick.

"I see you are as talented as you are lovely!" he said.

She glanced up at him briefly. He came close behind her, so close she could feel his body touch her bare shoulder.

"I must see you again," he said thickly, "I long to see your red hair trailing over those white shoulders of yours."

"Then you will be disappointed," Marisa said sharply.

"Listen, I tell you what I will do . . ." Lord Frederick began in a low voice, but before he could say more he was interrupted.

"Will you play bridge, Freddie?" the Duke asked.

He had approached the piano without Marisa being aware of it and now she wondered whether he thought she was encouraging Lord Frederick to single her out.

"His Royal Highness does not wish to play at the moment," the Duke continued, "but Brookie wants to make up a table and I am sure you would like to join him."

"Of course," Lord Frederick replied.

He walked away to where the bridge-tables had been set out with new packs of cards and markers arranged on the green baize.

Marisa went on playing.

She had the feeling, without raising her eyes, that the Duke was looking at her, but whether it was in condemnation as she had feared, she had no idea.

She played for another half an hour, and then to her relief she realised that the Prince who always liked to retire early had risen to his feet.

It was nearly midnight, and as the party was saying goodnight, Marisa moved towards the door. She had almost reached it when the Duke saw her.

"Good night, Miss Mitton," he said, "and thank you."

"Good night, Your Grace."

Marisa slipped past him.

She wondered if he was as angry with her as he had
been after Aline's misdemeanour in the Drawing-room
and then she was aware that Lord Frederick stood between her and the door.

"Good night, Miss Mitton," he said and held out his
hand.

She gave him hers. He held it very tight and she felt his
finger tickle her palm. She glanced at him and realised he
was looking at her in a meaningful manner.

It was nothing she could actually put into words, and
yet the impression was there and something in his protruding eyes and thick lips that made her suddenly afraid.

Pulling her hand away from his almost violently, she
hurried from the Drawing-room and out into the Hall.

She had reached the Grand Staircase when she changed
her mind and went along the corridor which led to another part of the Castle, and the gun-room.

Having found there what she sought, she went up the
back stairs.

Everything was quiet. There was still a fire burning
brightly in the School-room. She opened the door into
Aline's room.

Because she was afraid of the dark, the child always
slept with a night-light. Marisa could see her breathing
peacefully, well tucked up.

She went back into the School-room, leaving the bed-
room door ajar as she always did. She also left the door of
the School-room wide open and going into her own room
she locked the door.

She placed what she brought from the gun-room on top
of a chest. Then she walked across the room to stare at
herself in the mirror.

She looked at her red hair and the stars twinkling
against it, at the green gown which became her more than
anything she had ever worn before and she began to
laugh!

No wonder she had bewildered them. Who could expect
a governess to look like a bird of paradise?

But now the Ball was over, and Cinderella had gone

home. She certainly had no desire to be sought by Lord Frederick as he had suggested.

He was horrible, she thought, so horrible that all her contempt for Society engendered in her by her father seemed to surge up in a sudden disgust of him.

She wondered whether if she really had been a poor little governess from nowhere, she would have been beguiled or perhaps excited by Lord Frederick's compliments, his innuendoes, the manner in which he had tried to touch her.

Were there women who would welcome such things or rather be deceived by them, believing it to be a genuine interest, not just a passing lust!

Marisa took off her gown and hung it up in the wardrobe and then undressed. Her long hair, released from the pins, fell over her shoulders in a rippling fiery cloud.

She was just about to get into bed, when she heard a cry. At once she crossed the room and listened.

The cry came again, it was Aline.

Marisa put out her hand towards the door, then hesitated. She turned towards the chest on which she had set down something which she had brought from downstairs.

She picked it up, walked to the door and listened. There was no doubt that Aline was in distress.

"Help me . . . help me . . ."

Opening the door Marisa ran across the landing into the School-room. The room was almost in darkness and she paused for a moment to light the oil lamp which was set on the table.

It only took a few seconds for the golden light to fill the room, dispersing the shadows.

Then she went in to the child. Aline was having a nightmare. Marisa lit two candles, and putting her arms gently around the little girl held her close.

"It is all right, darling," she said, "wake up! You are only dreaming."

"Help . . . help," Aline cried, "she will . . . catch . . . me." Opening her eyes she exclaimed, "Oh, Miss Mitton, it was horrible! She was trying to . . . catch me . . . she was trying to . . . hit me with the . . . doll."

"You are dreaming, it is just a silly dream," Marisa said soothingly.

Aline gave a little sob.

"Look I am here," Marisa said, "and there is nobody else in the room."

"I thought . . . Lady Wantage was trying to . . . catch me," Aline murmured.

"She is very likely dreaming the same thing," Marisa suggested.

Aline gave a little laugh.

"I hope it is making her scream and cry too!"

Marisa could not help smiling.

"It is too late for you to be vindictive," she said. "Besides do not forget you are sorry you have been so naughty."

Aline snuggled against her.

"Tell me a story so that I can go to sleep again," she pleaded.

"I cannot. Do you remember, no stories for two days?" Marisa replied.

"It will seem a . . . very long . . . time," Aline complained.

"A punishment would not be any good unless one minded," Marisa replied.

She held Aline close and kissed the child's forehead as she spoke.

"If you read to me, it would not be the same as telling a story, would it?" Aline said shrewdly.

"We will talk about that tomorrow," Marisa answered. "Now go to sleep and no more silly dreams."

"Will you leave one of the candles?" Aline asked. "It is awfully dark in here even with the night-light."

"Yes of course I will leave it," Marisa replied, "but you are not to touch it, you know that?"

"No, of course not," Aline agreed, "I never touch candles."

"Then I will leave both of them alight," Marisa murmured, "but snuggle down in the bed clothes, so they will not keep you awake."

Aline did as she was told, she was in fact very dosy. Marisa tucked her in and waited for a little while until she heard the child breathing evenly and knew she was asleep.

Then very quietly she went from the room.

The School-room was bright with light from the oil lamp but it was only as Marisa closed Aline's door that she was aware of the fragrance of a cigar and saw Lord Frederick standing in front of the fire-place.

Instinctively she hid what she carried in her hand behind her back and then holding her wrapper stood looking at him.

"What do you want?" she asked in a low voice. "Or need I ask?"

"You know very well what I want," he replied.

As he spoke he threw his cigar into the fire.

"Your hair is even lovelier than I thought," he said thickly, "strands of silk in which to entwine a man's heart so that he cannot escape."

"Go away, Lord Frederick," Marisa said, "you have no right to come here, as you well know."

"When a woman looks as attractive as you, my dear," Lord Frederick replied, "you must expect a man to pursue you, and pursue you with ardour."

He walked towards her as he spoke, as he reached the table Marisa brought from behind her back the pistol she had collected from the gun-room when she came upstairs.

"You are making a mistake, Lord Frederick," she said and her voice was contemptuous. "You may find women who welcome attentions from a man who enjoys lechery without responsibility, but I can assure you that I am not one of them! Either you leave this room immediately, or I shall shoot you."

"You are bluffing!" Lord Frederick declared, but he had stopped still and there was a wary look in his eyes.

"I am not bluffing," Marisa answered, "and I am a good shot. I shall not kill you, for I have no desire to hang for someone as despicable as you. But I shall shoot you in the leg which will make it impossible for you, for the next few months at any rate, to climb two flights of stairs in pursuit of some wretched creature who would be too frightened to complain of your odious attentions."

"You are being ridiculous," Lord Frederick said. "A kiss and a cuddle hurt no-one, and I will teach you about love far better than the type of young man with whom you doubtless spend your days off."

"You are mistaken if you think I would appreciate anything that you could teach me," Marisa retorted. "And now get out before I lose my temper."

She spoke sharply raising her voice a little.

At that moment there was a step on the landing and almost before she had finished speaking, the Duke appeared in the open doorway.

It seemed to Marisa that he took in at one glance the situation in the room. Then he said quite calmly, his voice almost devoid of expression:

"Oh, here you are Freddie! I thought perhaps you might have lost the way to your room. I am afraid you are on the wrong floor."

The two men looked at each other for a long moment. Then Lord Frederick capitulated.

"How kind of you, Valerius!" he remarked and there was only a hint of sarcasm in his words. "I must admit to finding the Castle extremely bewildering."

"I thought that might be the explanation," the Duke said.

He stood on one side of the doorway to allow Lord Frederick to precede him who walked with quite a credible assumption of dignity from the room.

The Duke paused for a moment. He looked back at Marisa.

There seemed to her there was nothing but contempt in his eyes as they flickered over the muslin wrap which covered her night gown and at her hair fiery and glorious falling over her shoulders.

"It might be more effective, Miss Mitton," he said coldly, "and certainly less dramatic, if you locked your bed-room door."

With that he was gone, leaving Marisa so angry that she almost contemplated firing a bullet after him. She stormed into her bed-room, closed the door, locked it and flung down the pistol.

How dare the Duke assume that she had not been locked in! That she had not taken every precaution to prevent a scene such as had just been enacted!

If Aline had not had a nightmare, Lord Frederick could have knocked and battered on her door with no effect, she would not have answered him.

Then there would have been nothing that he could do but retire defeated.

She wondered if the Duke had noticed the way Lord Frederick had attempted to flirt with her all through dinner. She had thought him far too engaged with Lady Wantage even to glance in her direction.

Perhaps he might have been suspicious when Lord Frederick had come to the piano when she was playing.

Had the Duke made an excuse to go to his friend's room and finding it empty, had suspected where he might be found?

It was all a case of supposition and she had nothing to prove her point, she only knew that once again the Duke had humiliated her and put her in a position where she must be on the defensive.

It was obvious she could do nothing right where he was concerned.

First he had found Aline shooting a pheasant out of season, there had been the child's behaviour to Lady Wantage, and now this!

It was enough to make her feel that her dismissal from the Castle was predestined. She might as well pack her bags at once before he actually commanded her to go.

Then Marisa thought of Aline and knew that she would not give up so easily. How could she bear to leave the child at this moment when she had in fact changed her whole life?

Besides, before she went, she had something of importance to tell the Duke.

Marisa walked across her room and back. She thought she could never forget the scorn in the Duke's voice when he had spoken to her, when he had told her to lock her door.

Did he really credit that she had been waiting upstairs undressed for bed with her hair unbound, to receive a man like Lord Frederick?

Were all men so conceited that they thought that a woman had nothing better to do than to wait and hope for their attentions?

"I hate him!" Marisa said aloud.

Yet it was not so much hate which seethed inside her, but a feeling of resentment because she had been misunderstood, because, it seemed to her, the Duke was deliberately critical and censorious of everything she did.

She felt so agitated and upset by what had occurred, she knew it was no use getting into bed. Instead she made up the fire and sat down in front of it on the hearth-rug.

The warmth of the flames gradually dispensed a little of the cold hardness which seemed to lie within her breast.

She had told her aunt that her heart was frozen, that was true enough, but it did not prevent her feeling, when she was angry, as if something within her was struggling for existence and the very effort was painful.

"I hate him! I hate him!" she said again, and tried to tell herself that the scorn in his voice and the contempt in his eyes were not of the least importance.

She sat in front of the fire until it began to die down and she was suddenly conscious of feeling cold. She heard the stable clock strike the hour. It was three o'clock!

Marisa rose to her feet feeling cramped and started to take off her wrapper. As she did so, she heard a sound outside in the drive.

She wondered who it could be and, feeling curious, went to the window.

There was a bright moon and the sky was filled with stars. The Park and the lakes in the moonlight were very beautiful, so beautiful that for a moment Marisa stared at them almost spellbound until again she heard a sound below.

She looked and to her astonishment saw turning on the gravel beneath her window, a phaeton driven by a man in a top-hat. Beside him, rather cramped in the front seat were two other men, both wearing bowlers on their heads.

The horses drew up with a flourish and a groom jumped down from behind the phaeton to run to their heads.

The driver dismounted slowly and then as he went to walk towards the door, Marisa saw him clearly in the moonlight.

There was no mistaking the angle at which he wore his hat or the large moustache stretching out on either side of his thin face.

From where she stood, Marisa could also see the yellow

carnation in his button hole which matched the yellow body of the phaeton with its black wheels.

It was Lord Wantage! She had seen him characterised often enough and heard Miss Whitcham describe him as she laughed about his huge moustache and his penchant for yellow.

" 'Waspie Wantage' he is called," Miss Whitcham had laughed, "and Waspie by nature from all I hear!"

Fascinated, Marisa watched Lord Wantage walk up the steps to the front door. The two men in bowler hats followed him respectfully and she wondered who they might be. Suddenly she knew!

Only Lord Wantage could have thought of arriving at Vox Castle in the middle of the night with two detectives!

Just for one moment she thought it would serve the Duke right. He would get his just deserts when Lord Wantage, accompanied by his witnesses, discovered him in Her Ladyship's bed-room.

Then almost like a flash of lightning, Marisa's brain told her it must not happen, not with the Prince of Wales in the house and Mr. Arthur Balfour.

She could see the scandal which would result from Lord Wantage bringing a case for divorce against his wife and citing the Duke as co-respondent.

There would be headlines in every newspaper. The whole press would condemn not only the Duke, but also the Prince because yet another friend of his was in trouble.

His Royal Highness might even be sub-poenaed as a witness in the case, and Marisa was quite certain that Lord Wantage with his love for publicity would not spare either his future King or his friends if it suited him to punish his wife and her lover.

Suddenly Marisa knew what she must do.

Trembling she pulled her wrapper closely around her, unlocked the door and ran down the stairs.

It was a long way to the Grand Staircase and beyond to where the Duke's suite and Lady Wantage's faced each other across a wide corridor.

As Marisa reached the top of the Grand Staircase she heard the Night-Watchman moving slowly across the Hall

in answer to the front door bell that was being pealed con-
tinuously by Lord Wantage.

Marisa hurried across the landing and down the corridor. She knew where the Duke slept and she stopped at
the door opposite his.

She knocked. There was no reply! She knocked again.

It was then she heard the murmur of voices on the
other side of the corridor and she knew that Lady Wantage must have gone to the Duke's bed-room.

Just for a moment Marisa hesitated, before with a sense
of urgency she rapped on the door. There was silence.

Then the Duke's voice asked sharply:

"What is it?"

"Lord Wantage and two detectives have arrived, Your
Grace," Marisa answered breathlessly. "They are coming
upstairs at this moment."

There was a shrill cry, but Marisa did not wait to hear
more. She turned and sped back the way she had come.

As she reached the top of the staircase she saw that
Lord Wantage and the two men following him were already nearing the landing.

Keeping to the shadows Marisa slipped into the darkness of a doorway. Then she looked back.

Far away at the end of the corridor she saw a shadowy
figure leave the Duke's room and pass through a door opposite.

She gave a little sigh of relief, then slowly, without hurrying, she began to climb the stairs back to the School-
Room floor.

Chapter Six

The Duke bade goodbye to the last of his guests and then as the carriages moved away down the drive he said to the Butler:

"Order Samson immediately."

Twenty minutes later galloping over the Park he felt such a sense of freedom that it was as if he had been suddenly liberated from prison.

The last three days had been almost unbearable.

Hating subterfuge, disliking to find himself in the part of a hypocrite, it had gone against the grain to greet Lord Wantage with surprise on Friday morning and during the whole weekend adroitly to avoid a scene with his wife.

Like all women, Hetty Wantage had wished to talk over what had occurred, to justify her ignorance of her husband's movements, and to make sure that somehow, although she had no idea how, the Duke would remain her lover.

In this the Duke was determined to disappoint her.

He realised that only by a hair's breadth had he escaped a scandal which would have reacted disastrously on all his friends and especially on the Prince of Wales.

He could hardly credit that he had been so stupid as not to have been suspicious of Lord Wantage's permitting his wife to come to Vox alone.

"Anyone but a nitwit," the Duke accused himself, "would have thought it peculiar."

He realised now that Lord Wantage was not the type of man to be cuckolded with impunity.

He would not mind the publicity of a divorce and in fact would enjoy the role of the injured husband, betrayed not only by his wife, but by a very distinguished member of the social world in which they both moved.

"His nick-name is apt," the Duke muttered to himself.

But he knew that while Lord Wantage's action in bringing two detectives with him in the middle of the night to the house of a friend might be condemned by his Peers, he would certainly have received the sympathy of respectable middle-class Victorian England.

"How could I have been such a fool?" the Duke asked himself for the thousandth time.

He spurred Samson on to a gallop, and the speed at which he rode removed the last of the intolerable tension from which he had been suffering.

When he reached the boundary of the Park, the Duke drew a deep breath of the crisp October air and guided the stallion through a small plantation towards a gallop which was ideal for trying out the paces of any horse.

Constructed by his father, the gallop had however sunk into disuse when the Duke had moved his stud to Newmarket.

His Grace was therefore surprised, as he came to the edge of the plantation, to see two horses coming towards him at speed.

As they drew nearer he saw the smaller horse carried what appeared to be a jockey on its back. Then as it approached, he realised it was not a boy who was riding it but his daughter.

She was astride a horse which he would have thought was too big for her. With a velvet jockey-cap on her head and bending forward as she must have seen the grooms do in the effort to increase the pace of her mount, she was riding, the Duke had to admit, extremely well.

A little behind Aline, having obviously given the child a good start, came Marisa, on a spirited horse with a touch of Arab in his breeding.

She was riding superbly and with an expertise that told the Duke she was no novice.

She was wearing a dark habit—it was old but fitted her well. Lady Barrington's gifts had not included any riding gear.

There was a white gauze jabot at her throat, which was

echoed by the white gauze veil which encircled her high-crowned hat and floated out behind her as she galloped.

Her red hair in its neat chignon was a vivid patch of colour as she passed the Duke without seeing him, intent on watching the child a little ahead of her.

Then as they reached what the Duke could see was a roughly constructed winning-post with a small white handkerchief on top of a stick, Marisa moved her horse up a few paces until the two animals passed it neck to neck.

"I won! I won!" the Duke heard Aline cry as they drew their horses to a standstill.

They cantered to the end of the gallop and then turned to come back. They were soon in earshot and the Duke heard Aline say again:

"I won, didn't I, Miss Mitton?"

"By a nose," Marisa replied with a smile.

"And I handled Kingfisher well?"

"Very well indeed. You are improving every day."

"Do you think Papa . . ." Aline began.

She stopped speaking as she saw the Duke. He came from between the trees and rode onto the ride.

He moved towards them, raising his hat to Marisa, and said coldly to Aline:

"You rode as I would expect a groom or a stable-boy to ride."

Aline could hear the rebuke in the words and the light went from her eyes. The Duke turned his head towards Marisa, but before he could speak she said:

"I have an explanation, Your Grace, which I would prefer to give you privately. Shall Aline and I continue our ride, or would you wish us to return immediately to the Castle?"

Her voice was icy in its coldness and belied the flushed colour in her cheeks and the tiny curls which had escaped from the severity with which she had dressed her hair.

"Finish your ride by all means, Miss Mitton," the Duke replied. "I will see you in my Study after luncheon."

He raised his hat again and cantered away down the gallop. Both Marisa and Aline were silent as they watched him go.

There was something awe-inspiring about such a big man on such a magnificent stallion.

"He seems part of the horse," Marisa murmured almost to herself.

"He was angry," Aline said in a low voice.

"Only because you are wearing breeches," Marisa answered. "I thought he would have left with the guests. But your divided skirt should arrive today, the tailor promised it over the weekend."

"I never thought Papa rode here," Aline said.

There was a note of disappointment in her voice which made Marisa feel like cursing the Duke.

It was always the same, she thought; whenever he appeared he took all the happiness from the child's face.

They rode on for another half an hour but their gaiety was quenched. Aline was quiet, and Marisa deep in her thoughts had little to say.

She had kept Aline away from the house-party ever since the disastrous episode with Lady Wantage.

Fortunately nobody had asked to see her. Marisa was quite certain that Lady Wantage, when the Duke was not present, had made the very most to the other guests of Aline's misdemeanour, blaming not only the child, but the governess who had no control over her.

She had learnt from Miss Whitcham all that was taking place.

There had been riding and driving on Friday. Saturday morning the gentlemen, except the Prince, went out shooting at 10-30 a.m. returning for tea in the gold and white Drawing-room.

There the ladies were waiting for them like lovely butterflies in gorgeous brightly coloured tea-gowns.

After tea of hot buns, home-made jam and jersey cream, Gentleman's Relish, anchovey and asparagus sandwiches, fruit-cake, seed-cake, Madeira, cherry, walnut and chocolate cakes, everyone returned to their bed-rooms to rest on a *chaise-longue* against lace pillows.

At seven o'clock the lady's maids were ready to lace their mistresses into their close-fitting corsets and fasten the tight-waisted, low-necked gowns with long trains.

Glittering with tiaras, necklaces, bracelets, earrings, and

finger-rings, they swept down to dinner like bejewelled swans. Everyone would be in bed by midnight.

"Lady Brooke at Easton Lodge," Miss Whitcham giggled, "always warns her visitors that the stable-yard bell rings at 6 a.m. So convenient!"

Marisa had known the Duke would not wish to discuss the matter of the mouse or anything else with her until his guests had departed.

She had hoped almost against hope, that he would go with them and she would then be spared what she knew would be a very unpleasant interview.

She could not help continually wondering if he was aware who it was who had warned him of Lord Wantage's arrival.

Would he have recognised her voice? She wished now that she had made some effort to disguise it.

Perhaps if she had spoken with a Scottish accent, he would have supposed it was one of the housemaids. She only hoped that if he did realise it was her, he would be diplomatic enough for both their sakes to pretend ignorance.

When finally luncheon was finished and Aline went to lie down on her bed, Marisa, feeling more like a schoolgirl than a teacher, went downstairs to the Study.

She had carefully chosen to wear her plain gown with its demure white collar and cuffs. She had swept her hair severely back from her forehead and pinned it into such a tight chignon that it hurt.

But because she was apprehensive her eyes were more vividly green than usual and her face very pale as she entered the Study.

The Duke was sitting at his desk. He looked up at her entrance and rose slowly to his feet.

"Come in, Miss Mitton," he said, "I think we have several matters to discuss."

Feeling as if it was an almost impossible effort to reach the chair on the other side of the desk, Marisa moved towards it conscious that the Duke's eyes were on her.

She seated herself bolt upright and clasped her hands in her lap almost like a child about to recite.

There was silence and then the Duke asked:

"Well, Miss Mitton, where do we begin?"

She fancied there was a hint of amusement in his voice.

Angrily she told herself he was deliberately making her feel uncomfortable, trying to put her at more of a disadvantage than she was already.

Because she felt a surge of rage she managed to say almost aggressively:

"Which explanation would you wish to hear first, Your Grace?"

"I suppose we might start with the mouse," the Duke replied.

"Aline is very sorry for what she did," Marisa said, "but Your Grace must forgive my impertinence if I suggest that it was not very wise of you, knowing what had happened to the doll, to ask Aline downstairs when you and Lady Wantage were alone."

As she expected, the Duke raised his eyebrows at her reply. Then he said quietly:

"I had no choice, Lady Wantage desired personally to give Aline the present she had brought with her. As she insisted, I could hardly say my daughter did not wish to receive her gift."

"I should have thought it was difficult—but not impossible," Marisa murmured.

"So I am to blame for what occurred?" the Duke asked.

"Your Grace will perhaps see that there were some extenuating circumstances in what, I admit, was Aline's extremely reprehensible behaviour."

"I am glad you agree on that," the Duke said. "And now may I ask you why my daughter must ride in what even those who are not strait-laced would consider an immodest manner?"

"Aline is only a child," Marisa said quickly.

"But old enough to shoot?" the Duke interposed.

She realised he had scored a point and continued:

"I found that while Aline has a natural aptitude for riding, for years she had only been allowed to do so on a leading-rein. It had made her feel insecure and apprehensive. I have always thought it difficult for a small girl to learn to control an animal riding side-saddle, therefore to increase Aline's confidence, I have allowed her to ride astride."

The Duke did not speak and Marisa went on:

"It is unfortunate that Your Grace should have seen her today. Tomorrow she will be wearing a divided skirt which I ordered to be made as quickly as possible. She will then appear more feminine and perhaps will gain a little favour in your eyes."

"You can hardly expect me to commend her for her behaviour on Thursday afternoon," the Duke said.

"One can be angry with a child," Marisa answered, "but that is not so hurtful as indifference."

"The indifference I habitually show my daughter?" the Duke asked and there was a cynical note in his voice which was unmistakable.

Marisa hesitated a moment and then, not looking at the Duke, her eye-lashes dark against her pale cheeks, she said:

"Aline is very like . . . you. She has the same . . . forthrightousness, the same . . . determination once she has made up her mind."

"So you really think she is like me?" the Duke questioned.

Now the cynicism in his voice was too bitter to be ignored.

"I think family characteristics are inescapable," Marisa replied.

She looked at the Duke for the first time and there was a challenge in her eyes as she went on:

"I have red hair like my mother, my grandmother and my great-grandmother. It runs in our family, only the women have it, the men are usually dark. The Verleys also have a family characteristic."

The Duke looked puzzled and Marisa continued:

"You must have noticed it so often in the portraits of your ancestors."

"I have no idea to what you refer," the Duke said casually as if he thought the conversation had wandered from the point.

Marisa rose from her chair.

"I want to show you something," she said.

She walked across the room. Without looking back she was aware that the Duke followed her reluctantly.

She stopped in front of the mantelpiece. Above it was a

portrait of the first Duke of Milverley painted by Van Dyke.

He wore the elaborate costume in fashion at the time of the restoration of Charles II and a dark wig curling to his shoulders framed a clever face with its clear-cut aristocratic features.

It was a magnificent painting. With Vox Castle in the background the Duke was depicted leaning negligently against an ornamental urn.

His left hand hung elegantly from beneath a lace cuff.

"Can you see that he has the same peculiarity as yourself?" Marisa asked quietly.

The Duke stared at his ancestor's portrait.

"Is this a puzzle?" he asked. "I suppose there is something in our features which is the same."

"Not in his face, but in his hand," Marisa answered. "How brilliantly Van Dyke painted hands, it is noticeable in all his portraits!"

The Duke looked more closely at the hand of the first Duke.

"And now look at your own," Marisa said.

He spread out his fingers, they were long, thin, well shaped.

"Are you still so blind?" Marisa asked.

"I am afraid you must enlighten me, Miss Mitton. I may be very obtuse, but I have no idea what you are trying to say," the Duke replied.

"Look at your first finger," Marisa said. "Do you not see that it is exactly the same length as the middle finger? That is very unusual. In most people's hands the first finger is shorter, like my own."

She held out her own hand as she spoke, placing it beside the Duke's. It was very small in comparison to his, but her fingers also were long and elegant.

As she had said, her first finger was considerably shorter than her middle finger.

"If you look at the pictures of your relatives which are all over the Castle," Marisa went on as the Duke stared down at his hand, "you will find that, where the artist has depicted the hands carefully, the index finger is always the same length as the one next to it."

She pointed toward the picture.

"Strangely enough it is apparently only on the left hand of the Verleys that this occurs," she went on. "Aline's left hand is exactly the same as yours. Her first finger is the same length as the next one and she even has the same filbert nails."

For a moment the Duke said nothing, he was still staring at his own hand. Then he asked and his voice seemed hoarse:

"Is this really true?"

"You can see the resemblance for yourself," Marisa answered.

"My God!" he spoke beneath his breath.

He walked away from her across the Study to stand staring out into the garden.

Marisa did not move. She knew he was looking in the darkness of his soul and realising that for nine years he had punished his own child because the woman to whom he had been married had wished to hurt and humiliate him.

The Duke was silent for so long that Marisa began to wonder if she should go quietly from the room.

Then he said, still with his back to her:

"How did you know the other night that Lord Wantage had arrived?"

There was a pause before Marisa answered in a low voice.

"I was awake, my bed-room looks out over the front, I heard him drive up in a phaeton."

"And how did you know he had brought detectives with him?"

"I . . . suspected that was what they . . . were," Marisa faltered. "I had heard that His Lordship had been . . . difficult about your . . . association with . . . Lady Wantage while you were staying at Dunrobin Castle."

The Duke turned round from the window, an expression of astonishment on his face.

"You heard that?" he queried. "How could you possibly have heard such a thing?"

Marisa looked at him for a moment before she answered.

"Your Grace cannot be so naive as to believe that anything about you is kept secret. Miss Whitcham was told of what had happened as soon as you arrived South."

"I cannot believe it!" the Duke exclaimed. "Are you honestly telling me that such intimate and personal matters are public knowledge?"

"Not exactly public," Marisa replied, "but though it may seem strange to you, servants are human beings. They talk, they gossip, and they are extremely interested in their betters!"

The Duke walked across the room and sat down again at his desk.

"You astound me, Miss Mitton," he said. "So you were expecting that Lord Wantage might appear."

"Indeed I was expecting nothing of the sort!" Marisa answered sharply. "Only when I saw him arrive ... I knew at once why he had ... come."

She moved slowly across the room to stand in front of the desk and the Duke looked up at her. His eyes seemed peculiarly penetrating.

"So you saved me," he said. "Why?"

Marisa's eyes flickered before his and without really meaning to she sat down in the chair. She somehow felt she must answer him and truthfully.

"I do not know the ... answer to that ... question," she hesitated, "it is something I have asked myself. I have ... hated you for the way you have treated Aline and ... for other reasons too ... and yet when I could have stood aside and watched you ... disgraced, I was unable to do so. Perhaps it was ... because I did not wish ... Aline to see her ... father ... discredited."

"You are very frank, Miss Mitton," the Duke said wryly

"You asked me!" Marisa replied defensively.

"Yes, I asked for the truth!" the Duke admitted. "Now I wonder how I can express my gratitude, and how too I can apologise for the behaviour of a man who, until now, I have thought of as a friend."

"There is no need for you to express your gratitude or to apologise for Lord Frederick," Marisa replied. "He behaved as I expected him to behave."

"So you took a pistol with you to bed!" the Duke replied. "Had he told you he was coming upstairs?"

"No, not in actual words," Marisa answered, "but I have heard so many tales of the manner in which in big houses governesses and even house-maids are treated by gentlemen of quality who have nothing better to do than to hunt defenceless women."

She spoke scornfully. Her eyes flashing as she spoke.

"You have good reason to condemn very forcibly what occurred the other night," the Duke said, "but I can only hope that you exaggerate if you think that many men in the social world would treat a woman in your position in such a manner."

"I understand it happens frequently," Marisa replied, "too frequently for one to dismiss what occurred on Thursday night as an isolated incident."

"I can only apologise most sincerely that it occurred under my roof," the Duke said, "and hope it will not prejudice you unduly."

"I can assure Your Grace that Lord Frederick's behaviour does not in any way alter my opinion of men," Marisa answered.

She spoke so violently that the Duke looked startled.

"You talk as if you despise my whole sex!"

"I do!" Marisa replied. "I despise men and I hate them!"

She spoke without considering her words and then added quickly:

"I am sorry, Your Grace . . . my private feelings can be of no . . . interest to you."

"I can assure you that they interest me very much," the Duke answered. "You hold a very important place in my household, Miss Mitton, and as you teach my daughter, obviously your feelings and your beliefs must be my concern."

"Aline up to now has found much to hate in her life," Marisa said quietly. "She has never known love, which is what I have been trying to tell you ever since I came to the Castle. I shall certainly not inflict upon her my own dislikes and prejudices, I promise you that."

She spoke with an unmistakable sincerity, her large eyes seeking his as if to convince him.

"And yet you will go on hating my sex" the Duke said slowly.

"How can I help myself?" Marisa asked.

"One day you will change your mind," the Duke said, "you will fall in love, Miss Mitton, and then you will find that a man is not such a despicable creature as you find him at the moment."

"I can assure Your Grace that will not happen," Marisa replied sharply.

"How can you be so sure?" the Duke asked with an amused note in his voice.

"I am sure!" Marisa answered positively. "Do you think I am interested in the nauseating, lecherous emotions expressed by men like Lord Frederick or even ..."

She stopped suddenly as she realised that, carried away by her violence, she was on the edge of being extremely rude.

"... or even by myself," the Duke finished.

Then suddenly, to Marisa's surprise, he banged his clenched fist on the table in front of him.

"Good God, woman, that is not love!" he said angrily. "Do you really imagine I am such a half-wit as to think a maudlin sentimentality, a flirtatious interlude, or a barely concealed lust is worthy of the name of love? Of course it is not!"

His voice was scornful.

"You must be intelligent enough to know that what I am speaking of is something quite different. I am speaking of real love. The love that a man and a woman find once in a life-time if they are fortunate, but which for the majority is only a dream which is eternally out of reach."

He spoke so forcibly that Marisa could only stare at him, wide-eyed in astonishment.

"Love, Miss Mitton," the Duke went on in his deep voice, "is something irresistible, something which no-one can control or avoid. It is an all-consuming fire. It is a tidal wave drowning one in a sea from which there is no chance of being rescued. It is an ecstasy that is half agony, half-rapture, and it is completely inescapable!"

His eyes were holding Marisa's and she felt mesmerised by the manner with which he spoke and the words which she had never expected to hear from him.

Then, as they looked at each other in a silence that seemed somehow to be poignant with meaning, the Duke rose to his feet and pushing back his chair walked again to the window.

"That is love, Miss Mitton," he said more quietly, "and I hope that one day you will find it."

Marisa stood up.

She felt a little breathless as if she was swimming against the tide in a tempestuous sea. The Duke's shoulders were very broad against the sunshine outside.

She felt suddenly there was so much she wanted to ask him, so much she wanted to hear; and yet she knew that he had finished with her, he had no more to say and she should go.

She stood irresolute. Then he said:

"I am going away this afternoon. I am shooting tomorrow with Lord Acton, but I shall be back on Tuesday evening. Tell Aline I will take her riding with me on Wednesday."

Marisa gave what was almost a little cry.

"Oh, I am glad!" she exclaimed. "Aline will be so thrilled."

"The invitation includes you both," the Duke said turning round. "I should like to race you on the gallop, Miss Mitton! I think it would be a satisfaction to beat you!"

"I am sure you could do that quite easily," she answered.

"Would it be so easy?" he asked. "I wonder."

Marisa had the feeling that their lips were saying one thing but they were talking about something quite different.

Then because she felt suddenly shy, she said quickly:

"Have you . . . finished with . . . me, Your Grace?"

"For the moment, Miss Mitton," the Duke replied.

She would have turned to go, but he moved to her side and unexpectedly took her hand in his.

"I have a great deal for which to thank you," he said, and unexpectedly he raised her hand to his lips.

She felt his mouth warm against the softness of her skin.

Then, as the colour flared into her face and she felt for some unaccountable reason that she could hardly breathe, she went quickly from the room without looking back.

It seemed to Marisa as if the rest of the day passed in a kind of dream.

She told Aline that her father had forgiven her and that they were to go riding with him on Wednesday and the child's excitement was pathetic.

Aline had innumerable questions to ask.

"Was he very angry with me, Miss Mitton? What did he say about my riding astride? Has he forgiven me for giving Lady Wantage a mouse?"

On and on, over and over again, Aline asked questions, until Marisa felt her head was buzzing.

They went for a walk but there was no escape from Aline's curiosity, and when finally the child was taken to bed, Marisa escaped to her own room with a sense of relief.

It was then she could ask herself exactly what had happened at her interview with the Duke. Her feelings were hard to understand.

She had hated him, and yet when she had proved to him that Aline was in truth his child, she had felt an intense compassion for the manner in which he had been deceived for over nine years.

How could any woman have done anything so inhuman as to deny him his fatherhood, to sentence her own child to the barrenness that had been Aline's life when she had been unwanted and disliked by her only surviving parent.

It was a cruelty that only a woman selfishly obsessed by her own emotions could have perpetrated.

Marisa felt that she loathed the unhappy Duchess who must have been in actual fact as mentally deranged as those who had known her affirmed.

"But I still hate the Duke," Marisa told herself. "He is typical of his class, and whatever he may say he is just as bad as his friends."

Yet somehow the words rang false.

She had tried to excite her anger against the Duke by remembering the foolishness and spitefulness of Lady Wantage. She tried to recall how she had loathed him when he had disparaged her years ago at her debutante ball.

But the fire had gone, and she could only feel instead a

strange but positive interest in the Duke, which had nothing to do with his love affairs in the past.

She could not help recalling how warmly Mr. Arthur Balfour had spoken of him, and all for the rest of the day the Duke's deep voice speaking of love as inescapable seemed to ring in her ears.

"I am mad!" Marisa berated herself. "He is a man and all men are contemptible!"

She thought of him kissing Lady Wantage and holding her closely in his arms as Lord Wantage drove up to the front-door.

"Why was I so stupid as to warn him?" Marisa asked aloud, "I should have let him be punished for his indiscretions. I should have let him bear the consequences of committing adultery with another man's wife."

But she had saved him, and she wondered how discomfited, and perhaps how disappointed, Lord Wantage had been when he found his wife alone in her own bed-room and being convincingly surprised to see him.

"They are all disgusting" Marisa said aloud.

But she knew it was upon Lady Wantage that she heaped her scorn, rather than upon the Duke.

When it was dinner-time she sent a message to Miss Whitcham to say she was tired and would not be dining with her tonight.

She felt she could not listen to the Secretary chattering about the house-party and being ready to speculate over and over again as to why Lord Wantage had arrived in the middle of the night.

The Night-Watchman had of course talked. On Friday morning everyone in the Castle knew that Lord Wantage had arrived with two strange men who having entered the house had left almost immediately and been driven away by his groom.

The only good thing was that no-one knew that Marisa had been in any way involved.

Miss Whitcham had assumed that either the Duke's love-making had finished before Lord Wantage's arrival, or else they had been really frightened by his attitude at Dunrobin Castle and had taken no chances.

"I cannot listen to any more" Marisa told herself.

Having had a very light meal in the School-room, she went to her own room intending to go to bed.

It was only 9 o'clock, and suddenly she decided to open her leather bag and bring out the manuscript at which she had not looked since she arrived at the Castle.

She spread it out on the hearth-rug in front of the fire. She did not know why, but now she had a sudden reluctance to read it.

She had written thousands of words incorporating large chunks of Aunt Augusta's diaries. She had also found several books in her father's Library which had been of help, but now she knew that there was so much more she could add from the Library downstairs.

She stared at the manuscript.

"I must finish it and then I can leave the Castle" she told herself and knew the idea was hurtful.

She had no wish to go but it was obvious she could not spend the rest of her life in the position of a governess.

Her aunt was right, it was a degrading and subservient position for someone like herself. She would go and live with Miss Meadfield her old governess, she would write.

Once this book was finished and was a success, it would be easy to get anything else published.

She felt a sudden desire to run away and not to see the Duke again, not to hear his voice talking of love.

She was afraid of him she thought, afraid in a very different manner from her previous fears, and it was a feeling she did not understand.

She picked up the manuscript and resolutely went downstairs. There was a lot more work to be done and the sooner it was completed the sooner she could leave.

The lights were on in the Library, the servants had grown used to her using the room until late at night.

Marisa put the manuscript down on the desk in the centre of the room and then climbed the ladder to the balcony.

There were a great many more facts she wanted about William IV and his ten illegitimate children by Mrs. Jordan and she was certain there would be some out-spoken books on the subject that her father did not possess.

Then as she moved along the balcony to where she

thought the books might be, she saw that in the French section there was a new book by Guy de Maupassant.

It was entitled "Fort comme la Mort" and she realised it had only just been published. The librarian could only have added it to the shelves in the last few days.

She picked it up with a feeling of delight.

There was no-one, she thought, who wrote better and she only wished she could emulate de Maupassant's vivid and brilliant style.

She opened the book meaning just to glance at the first page. Half an hour later she was so lost in what she was reading, she did not hear the door open or the Duke come in.

He had returned unexpectedly because his host had been taken ill and the shooting party had been cancelled.

He had driven back to the Castle and when he entered the Hall the Butler had informed him that Miss Mitton was in the Library.

His feet made no sound on the thick carpet.

He looked up, saw Marisa on the balcony and then as he was about to speak to her, he saw the manuscript lying on the table.

It was set out in several piles and almost without intending to do so the Duke read the page on the top of the pile nearest to him.

THE SCANDALS OF SOCIETY

A hundred years of depravity.

1. Love letters from The Prince of Wales to an actress.
2. The indiscretions at Carlton House.
3. Lord Nelson bewitched by Emma Hamilton.
4. Prostitutes, Parasites and Peers.
5. The ten bastards of William IV.

There were various other headings obviously each for a chapter in the manuscript. The Duke's eyes skipped over them to the end where he read:

20. The Prince of Wales' infatuation for Lily Langtry.
21. Licentiousness and the Marlborough House Set.
22. Cheating at Tanbury Croft.
23. The promiscuity of a Noble Duke.

The Duke must have made an involuntary exclamation for Marisa raised her head from the book and saw him.

Then she realised what he held in his hand and ran along the balcony, clambered down the staircase and came swiftly across the room.

"Put that down at once!" she cried. "You are not to read it . . . it is mine!"

The Duke stared at her with an expression of fury on his face.

"So that is what you are! A spy!" he said scathingly. "A mud-slinging snooper listening at the key holes! What newspaper is paying you for this filth?"

"No-one . . . it is not true" Marisa stammered. "I wrote . . . it for . . . myself."

"Do you expect me to believe that?" the Duke enquired. "You have wormed your way into my household merely so that you can uncover every filthy scandal, every defamatory insinuation about me and my friends. How dare you!"

"It is . . . not . . . true" Marisa protested.

"You lie" the Duke said, "I can see in your eyes you are lying, but now I know you for what you are—a muck-raker and a calumniator. You intend to slander my friends with a scurrilous malevolent book when they have no chance to defend themselves."

"No . . . no . . ." Marisa cried.

"You are lying again" the Duke stormed at her. "I thought you were different. I did not believe you were an ordinary governess, I thought there was some reason for your being here, but I had not suspected this."

His voice had risen and it seemed to Marisa as if he towered over her menacingly.

She was frightened and trembling as she stood in front of him, her eyes fixed on his face.

"This obscenity from the past" the Duke said scornfully indicating the manuscript, "and these scandals of the present, have you never thought for one moment in your poisonous little mind, that the reason men and women do such things is because they are unhappy?"

He stared at her as he continued.

"Has it never struck you that they are seeking something outside themselves, something they cannot find?

Many of the scandals over which you are licking your lips occur merely because through circumstances over which the parties concerned had little control, they were forced into marriage with someone for whom they had no affection."

His eyes were dark with anger as he continued.

"Can you not as a woman understand that such people are condemned to a life of misery and loneliness, except that love in some shape or form can make their existence a little more bearable. Have you thought of that as you hound and besmirch them?"

He seemed almost to spit the words at her and then as she stood quivering in front of him, her eyes wide with fear, her lips trembling, a very different expression came into his eyes.

"I respected you," he said savagely, "I believed you when you told me you hated men and were disgusted by them. But now I know that you were lying. Perhaps you enticed Lord Frederick to your bed-room merely so that you could have the satisfaction of recording his behaviour in your diary of sexual activities!"

"It is not . . . true!" Marisa cried, "it is not . . . true!"

"And you have flaunted your red hair and your white skin in front of me" the Duke continued his face contorted with anger, "how remiss of me not to play the part you expected of a Ducal libertine!"

Marisa tried to speak but her voice had died in her throat.

"We can of course make up for lost time" the Duke went on, "so here is something else to add to your bawdy chapters."

As he spoke, his voice bitter and sarcastic, he swept her roughly into his arms. She gave a cry because his action was so unexpected.

Then his lips were on hers and he was holding her so tightly that she could not breathe.

He kissed her brutally with a fury and an anger which bruised her mouth. She made an effort to struggle but she was completely impotent beneath his strength and her hands could only flutter futilely against his chest.

He kissed her lips until she believed she must faint from his violence.

Then he kissed her eyes, her cheeks and bending his head further, kissed the softness of her white neck.

"Please ... please let me ... go" she pleaded.

But his mouth silenced the words.

She felt as if a furnace of fire had opened suddenly and enveloped her with its burning heat.

She was frightened to the point where she could not even think but could only quiver beneath the hard passionate possessiveness of his lips.

No-one had ever kissed her before and she did not know that a man could hold a woman completely captive because his mouth possessed hers.

She knew the Duke's anger had made him lose control. But now some other emotion consumed him and it frightened her even more than his fury.

"Please ... please" she whispered again, aware that whatever he did she was too weak to fight him.

Suddenly the Duke released her.

"Damn you!" he stormed, "damn you! Get out of my sight!"

Then he was gone from the Library slamming the door behind him.

For a few seconds Marisa could only hold on to the desk feeling she must fall to the floor.

Then with a sob she gathered up the manuscript scattered on the desk and holding it tightly to her arms she ran from the Library and up the staircase to her own room.

Breathless she stopped for a moment inside the door, before crossing the floor she threw the manuscript into the fire.

The flames caught the pages of her careful writing and flared higher and higher until the sound of their burning roared up the chimney.

With a sob that seemed to shake her whole body Marisa flung herself down on the hearth-rug and burst into a tempest of bitter heartbreaking tears.

Chapter Seven

Marisa cried until she could cry no more and then, shivering with cold and misery, she undressed and got into bed.

In the darkness she found herself facing-up to what she had done and realising that the Duke was justified in what he had said to her.

How, she asked herself, could she have so lowered herself as to become in his own words—"a muck-raker and a calumniator"?

She had not believed it possible that a man should speak to her as the Duke had done, and yet she was honest enough to admit that he had every justification.

What he did not know, and what Marisa realised now for the first time, was that she had been just an instrument of her father's rancour and bitterness.

Looking back, she could remember when she was only five his saying to her:

"Always remember, Marisa, that men are foul and bestial. Avoid them, hate them, for they will pretend to be your friend and then stab you in the back."

She could see now how, because he had few friends and no-one else to talk to, her father conversed with her as if she were a man and his contemporary.

It was to her that he raged against Society, attributing to its members every vice, every depravity, and she was too young to understand that in reality it was only one man that he indicted—Lord Geltsdale.

It was her father who, as she grew older, had suggested that she write to the newspapers and magazines, and then had put into her head the idea of writing a book.

He might have done it himself but once he had a pen in his hand, his style became heavy and pompous.

When Marisa discovered Great Aunt Augusta's diaries and showed them to him, he had exclaimed.

"Interesting, very interesting, Marisa! Why do you not turn them into a pamphlet, or better still a book? There was so much scandal at the time your Great Aunt Augusta scribbled down these daily observations in her life, that it should prove instructional reading for future generations."

He had paused and went on with a glint in his eye:

"The Bucks, the Dandies, the Rakes with whom George IV both as Prince of Wales and Regent consorted were so dissolute that their lives should be a warning to all decent-minded people."

"I suppose there are books to tell us what they did," Marisa had said, feeeling that she was lamentably ignorant about such matters.

"I will find you books," her father had answered, "and you can continue describing the behaviour of Society right up to the present day. Our so called noblemen have ruined the country. They should, every man Jack of them, be hung from the lamp-posts."

He had spoken with a kind of repressed fury which Marisa knew meant he was suffering.

She had been too young to realise, she thought now, that he fed his own misery and loathing of Lord Geltsdale with every scandal, every disreputable anecdote that could be described about the social world in which his wife's seducer had moved.

It was only now, with her tear-stained face against the pillow, that Marisa began to realise the truth.

Her father's Radical views, his often expressed sympathy for the miners, industrial workers, the aged and the poor were simply brick-bats he could fling at the aristocrats who ignored them or the employers who exploited them.

He had had no real feeling for the underdog; he did not really care who suffered.

He himself could concentrate on only one aim—the destruction of the social structure.

"How foolish I have been not to realise this," Marisa told herself.

She had always felt a deep resentment that her mother

had run away and left her, yet now for the first time, she began to feel that perhaps her mother could plead extenuating circumstances.

Beautiful and with a naturally passionate nature, at seventeen she had married a man twenty years older than herself, who was a scholar, a recluse who disliked, even in those days, being involved in the normal activities of Society.

Her parents, delighted at the thought of her marrying a distinguished man of sensible age who owned an ancient title and who was comparatively well off, had accepted the Earl's advances with alacrity.

They pushed their daughter up the aisle before she realised that the excitement of being the bride of such a man would soon disperse in the boredom of being his wife.

Marisa had heard the servants talking of how her mother had loved to dance, how she had wished to go hunting, and was seldom permitted to do either.

The Earl disliked both dancing and hunting. He went shooting but he did not ask his wife to accompany him.

It was only later, when he treated Marisa as if she was a son, that he taught her to shoot and took her with him walking miles around the Estate in search of game.

He must always have been austere, Marisa thought, a man who found it hard to express his feelings, and perhaps was incapable of very deep emotions except when he was aroused to hatred.

He had, she was sure, not tried to share his interests to his bride, or perhaps she had been too much in awe of him to suggest that he should do so.

Anyway after six years of boredom when Lord Geltsdale, only a few years older than herself, had come into her life, it was obvious that she had been unable to resist him.

They had first met out hunting, and when the summer came they had continued to meet secretly, Marisa's mother escaping daily from the dull gloomy house, leaving her indifferent husband immersed in his books.

He had been quite unaware of what was occurring until it was too late.

She must have loved Lord Geltsdale very deeply, Marisa thought, and remembered the Duke saying that love was "irresistible" and "completely inescapable".

How did he know so much about it, she wondered and remembered that he too had endured an unhappy marriage.

She tried to think of him suffering as her father had suffered, and now for the first time the people she had wished to lampoon became real, not just puppets known only from a printed page, without flesh or blood in them.

She remembered extracts from Great Aunt Augusta's diaries:

"Lord X came home last night and found Sir F . . . J . . . in his wife's boudoir. He challenged him to a duel and this morning at dawn left Sir F . . . J . . . wounded and on the point of death. Lord X has fled to France until the scandal shall blow over. Her Ladyship was always an emotional female and in my opinion the marriage was doomed from the out-set. But of course it was from her point of view an excellent match."

Marisa thought how she had been interested in the duel.

She had never, until now, thought of the agony the lady in question must have suffered when she was left alone, her lover dead, her husband in exile on the continent.

Had the love she felt for Sir F . . . J . . . been so intense that she felt that her life too was over and there was nothing left for her in the future?

Marisa could also remember her father showing her a coarse satirical cartoon of Lady Hamilton and Lord Nelson.

Yet the great British hero had a deep and real love for one of the loveliest women the world had ever seen. When he died he left the care of her to the country he had served so well.

There were so many ways how one could look at scandals and indiscretions.

"You can pillory George IV in your book" her father had said gloatingly. "He was a gross man with few virtues."

"But was that the truth?" Marisa asked herself in the darkness.

George IV had been a very cultured man, witty and with exquisite taste.

Did not the fact that he had always sought the companionship of older women show that he had missed in his boyhood the love and understanding of his parents?

As to William IV, on whose love-life with Mrs. Jordan she had expended a whole chapter, had he not behaved as a simple country gentleman might have done, living quietly at Bushey with the woman he loved but was unable by law to marry?

When eventually he came to the throne he heaped favours on their children, illegitimate indeed, but whom he loved dearly, giving them titles and finding them positions at Court.

"There are always two sides to a picture", Marisa could remember Miss Meadfield saying to her.

Looking back over her childhood, she realised that it was her governess who gave her the stability and the sense of reality that she never found in her father.

It was Miss Meadfield who taught her about nature.

The older woman came from country stock and while being exceptionally well read and a linguist, which was unusual, she had a real love for the countryside.

She would take Marisa for long walks and teach her about the trees, the flowers and the shrubs just as Marisa in her turn had tried to impart such knowledge to Aline.

Because Marisa was lonely and because an only child can find companionship only with her imagination, she peopled Miss Meadfield's beautiful simple world with fairies and elves, dragons and even, although she felt slightly guilty at doing so, with Knights in shining armour.

Yet she must be truthful and admit, having always liked honesty, that the research for the book that her father had suggested to her had been fun.

She loved books. She enjoyed the feel of them between her hands, to know the excitement of turning over the pages wondering what new bit of information she would find, what fresh knowledge was hidden away in the small print.

But when she was making notes of the scandalous

events she discovered as she sat at her desk in her father's study, it never struck her that she was playing with the lives of real people or that the characters of whom she wrote could suffer as deeply as she herself was suffering at this moment.

"Have you never thought for one moment in your poisonous little mind, that the reason men and women do such things is because they are unhappy?"

She could hear the anger in the Duke's voice as he stormed at her. Even to remember his words made her whole body tremble.

No, she had never thought that! She had just copied down what she had read like a pupil in the class-room.

She could see now she would never become a good writer however docilely she had set down the ideas that her father had suggested.

How could she write about matters of which she knew nothing? How could she describe or even imagine feelings that she had never felt?

What she had transcribed was just a mass of words. Words already written by someone else, sentences copied out from book after book and having little meaning save as an offering to the idol of malice and hatred at whose feet her father worshipped.

Yet she and no-one else had copied out those unsavoury slanders which had drawn the Duke's wrath down upon her.

If there was not enough humiliation in the way he had spoken to her—he had kissed her.

She could hardly credit now that she had not been able to struggle more fiercely against him when he had held her captive in his arms.

He had rained his kisses on her lips, her eyes and cheeks, so brutally that they were bruised and still hurt.

He had hated her, he despised and loathed her for the sins she had committed, and furthermore he had punished her with his kisses.

"Here is something else to add to your bawdy chapters" he had stormed.

Then finally when he had kissed her until she was almost insensible, he had flung her from him.

"Damn you, damn you, get out of my sight."

She could hear the roughness of his voice echoing in her ears, and she could feel a humiliation so intense that the mere memory of it brought the tears again to her eyes.

She had meant to leave the Castle eventually, but not like this, not creeping out like a pariah, something the Duke would always remember as foul and unclean.

"Oh God how can I make him understand" Marisa whispered, "how can I make him see that I did not mean to do it?"

She knew she never could explain the whole circumstances which had led up to doing what her father had asked of her and searching through his Library for the scandals of the past.

But she had to admit, if she was honest, that she had intended to write about the Duke.

She had hated him because of what he had said on that ghastly, unhappy Ball, when no-one had wished to dance with her and the young men, once they had done their duty, had hurried away in search of more attractive females.

She had hated him and yet been disturbed by him.

There was something in his deep voice which she could never forget. It was that which made her search through the magazines for photographs of him.

It was those, when she had found them, which made her store up all references to Vox Castle, long before she went there.

The Duke's handsome cynical face had, Marisa felt, been etched indelibly on her mind since the first moment she saw a picture of him.

And she could not forget his voice because over and over again she could hear him comparing her laughingly to a carrot.

She had hated him then with a ferocity that almost equalled her father's eternal tirade against Society.

When she had actually seen him, so large, so strong, towering above her on the great black stallion, a frown between his eyes, his lips tight set in anger, her heart gave a frightened leap, and she told herself that this was exactly as she knew he would be.

"Yet when I told him about Aline I was sorry for him," she whispered.

It was true she had felt a compassion she had never known before, as the Duke walked away from her to stand staring blindly out of the window in the Study.

She had realised how much he must have suffered because he believed in all sincerity that his wife had deceived him and he had fathered another man's child.

Marisa remembered that her aunt had said that the Duke had been tricked into marriage.

Was that true? Had some ambitious clever mother manoeuvred him into a position when the only honourable thing to do was to propose marriage?

Mrs. Featherstone-Haugh had often affirmed how easy it was, for a man to be caught by one of the designing Mamas who were determined to capture a social parti for their daughters.

"No wonder bachelors prefer the society of married women" Mrs. Featherstone-Haugh had added with a laugh. "Matrimonial vultures lie in wait for them like evil birds of prey. And if a man should as much as dance twice with an unmarried girl, it practically constitutes a proposal of marriage; while to walk alone with her in the garden, or to be found conversing with her in an empty room, is an action which drives him to the altar whether he wishes it or not!"

Could the Duke have been caught in such a manner, Marisa questioned?

Then she wondered if perhaps his bride had been as reluctant as he was to have their lives joined in holy matrimony?

It was all so complicated, so difficult to understand and yet she knew the Duke must have been speaking of himself when he had said:

"Many of the scandals over which you are licking your lips occur merely because through circumstances over which the parties concerned had little control, they were forced into marriage with someone for whom they had no affection."

That was what had happened to him and because of it he had grown deeply cynical. There was no mistaking the hardness of his eyes and the deep lines that ran from nose to mouth.

They came, Marisa was sure, because a man had lost

faith in life and had no hope that the future would prove
any different from the past.

"But there must be hope for him!" Marisa murmured to
herself.

She recalled again the violence of his lips on hers, the
manner in which his arms had encircled her so that it was
impossible to move and almost impossible to breathe.

He had been so angry, so incensed by her and yet he
had wished to touch her. She could have understood if he
had hit her, but instead he had kissed her!

She felt herself tremble at the thought, and then heard
again his voice ringing out with fury:

"Damn you, damn you, get out of my sight."

She had to leave the Castle. There was no doubt of that.
If she did not leave of her own free will, doubtless the
Duke would throw her out.

She must leave Vox, she must leave Aline . . . she must
leave . . . him!

Marisa gave a little sob and as she did so she knew the
truth!

She did not wish to go. It brought a pain such as she
had never endured before to realise that within a few
hours she would leave and never see the Duke again.

At the same time she suddenly knew why the thought
was so deeply hurtful. She loved him!

Of course it was love she felt for him! This pain, this
anguish within herself as if someone drove a sword between her breast . . . was love.

He had warned her but she had not believed him. He
had said love was "an all-consuming fire, a tidal wave
drowning one in a sea from which there is no chance of
being rescued".

That was what she was experiencing and it was so
much more tumultuous, so much more intense than he
had given her to believe.

She loved him!

It seemed impossible and yet she knew now although
she had been frightened by the violence of his kisses and
the roughness in which he had held her close against him,
she had not felt revolted or even insulted.

She had been frightened because she had never been
kissed before.

She had not known that a man's lips could be so brutal or that she would feel so weak and utterly helpless in his arms, and yet now the very thought of him made her quiver.

She felt something flicker within her like a flame lit from the fire that had been in his eyes. She loved him!

She had loved him long before she came to Vox—only she had thought it was hatred!

She loved him when they first talked together about Aline and later when he had explained to her the meaning of love.

It was not compassion which had seemed like a warm light within her when she told him that Aline was his child—but love.

A love which had wanted to sweep away the bitterness which his wife's lie had made fester within him for over nine years.

Marisa knew now that she had wanted to run across the Study, put her arms round the Duke and beg him to forget the past.

She had felt a sudden surging tenderness and maternal affection within herself for the man who had suffered so unjustly. But she had been too inexperienced and too shy to recognise it for what it was.

"Love! Love! Love!" she repeated the words over and over again in the darkness and knew that it was unlikely that she would ever see the Duke again.

There would be no goodbyes, no gratitude for the service she had been able to do him.

Even if he wished in courtesy to thank her again for saving him from the Divorce Courts, she knew she could not face the condemnation in his eyes, the scorn and contempt on his face or the bitterness of his lips.

Driven by a sudden urgency to be gone, Marisa sat up in bed and tried to plan what she would do.

She could not, she thought, bear to tell Aline that she was leaving, it would upset the child. She was sure Aline would cling to her and beg her not to go.

Such a scene would be unfair on Aline and unbearable from her own point of view. She must be more subtle than that.

She had an idea that Miss Whitcham had mentioned

that any train travelling towards London could be stopped at the Halt for Vox Castle if the signal was raised by the Duke's servants.

"I will send Aline riding" Marisa decided.

She heard the stable-clock strike five and getting out of bed she drew back the curtains. It was still dark and Marisa lit the candles on the dressing-table.

Then she started to fold her clothes that were to be packed and put them in neat piles on the bed so it would not take long to place them in her trunks once they were brought to her room.

"I must be careful', she thought, 'not to let Aline see my baggage or she will be suspicious'.

By half after seven o'clock Marisa had arranged everything tidily, washed and dressed herself.

Leaving her room she carefully closed the door behind her and went into the School-Room.

Gladys, the maid who cleaned the School-Room, was lighting the fire in the grate.

"You are early, Miss!" she exclaimed as Marisa walked in.

"Yes Gladys" Marisa replied, "and I want to speak to you."

She glanced at Aline's door as she spoke making sure that it was firmly shut so that they could not be overheard.

"Listen, Gladys," Marisa began, "I have to leave unexpectedly and I do not wish Her Ladyship to be upset. As soon as we have had breakfast, I will send her out riding and will arrange for one of the grooms to go with her. The moment she has gone downstairs, I wish you to fetch two of the footmen and tell them to bring my trunks to my bed-room."

Gladys looked apprehensive and she added:

"Ask one of the housemaids to help you and you will find all my things lying on my bed already folded. All you have to do is to put them into the trunks and get them carried downstairs. I shall leave to catch a train as soon as they are ready."

"Very good, Miss" Gladys replied, "but it'll upset Her Ladyship no end. Why, we were only saying yesterday how she fair dotes on you. You being here had made a real difference to her."

Gladys paused, then added with an anxious look in her eyes:

"You'll be coming back, Miss, won't you?"

"I do not know how long I shall have to be away," Marisa answered.

As she spoke she wished with all her heart that one day she could return.

Then she knew it was impossible! This was the end, this was the finish to a chapter in her life and there would be no turning back the pages.

Afraid that Gladys might see the unhappiness in her face, she walked to the bed-room door and opened it. Aline was sitting up in bed reading a book.

"Oh how lovely it is you, Miss Mitton!" she exclaimed, "I thought it must be Nanny coming to dress me."

"She will be coming soon" Marisa replied. "Would you like me to help you this morning?"

"Will you?" Aline asked, "I would like that, though I expect Nanny will be jealous!"

"Well perhaps we can surprise Nanny by having you ready and dressed by the time she gets here" Marisa suggested.

Aline put down her book, scrambled up on the bed and held out her arms.

"Look!" she cried, "I'm a fairy flying towards you."

She gave a great jump as she spoke and reaching Marisa's side, flung her arms round her neck.

"I love you, Miss Mitton," she said. "I woke up thinking of all the wonderful stories you're going to tell me."

"You will have to go riding first," Marisa answered, "and, Aline, would you mind very much if Hanson took you or one of the grooms? I have a headache."

"Oh poor Miss Mitton! I am sorry."

"Thank you, Aline."

"It would make your headache worse if you were bumping about in the saddle, wouldn't it?"

"I am afraid it would," Marisa agreed, "so I will send a message to the stables and tell a groom to accompany you."

"I would rather stay with you," Aline said.

"Oh no you would not!" Marisa contradicted, "you would find it very dull and you know how much you enjoy riding. Besides you must practise hard today so your father will be particularly impressed at how well you ride when he takes you out with him tomorrow."

"I am looking forward to that" Aline smiled, "do you really think Papa will approve of my new divided skirt?"

"I am sure he will," Marisa answered.

But she remembered with a little stab of her heart how the Duke had asked her to go with them before he had realised how despicable and two-faced she was.

"You do not look well, Miss Mitton," Aline exclaimed, unusually perceptive as Marisa helped her into her clothes.

"It is just my headache," Marisa replied.

She wondered if the child would understand if she told the truth and said it was a heartache from which she was suffering.

Marisa gave Aline her breakfast and although she could eat nothing she forced herself to talk amusingly and tell Aline things that she hoped the child would remember.

She had the wild idea that she could cram into one short hour all the things she wanted Aline to know for the rest of her life.

She felt herself yearn over the little girl and wondered if her affection was intensified because she was the Duke's child. No, she thought, she loved Aline for herself.

She loved the warm nature that had been frustrated and twisted by being treated in the wrong manner for so many years.

Yet only a superficial damage had been done. Beneath the tantrums, the aggressiveness and the sulks, was a warm heart and a generous nature.

"You will remember to thank Hanson or whoever takes you out riding?" Marisa said urgently.

"Of course I will," Aline answered. "I always thank people since you told me to do so. As I was coming up the stairs yesterday I heard one of the housemaids say to Miss Whitcham, 'that child has very pretty manners these days!' "

"I have always been told that listeners hear no good of themselves" Marisa smiled, "so you were lucky."

"I am always going to have pretty manners to everyone except Lady Wantage," Aline said.

Marisa just looked at her and she added in a rather shame-faced manner.

"Well . . . I will not be rude to her . . . again. Although I do not promise to be . . . very, very polite."

It was nearly 10 o'clock before Marisa took Aline downstairs to the front door where her horse was waiting.

Marisa saw that in answer to her message it was not Hanson the Head groom that was accompanying Aline, but a younger man called Jim whom the child liked and to whom she could chatter more easily than to the older man who had been at the Castle over thirty years.

"Look after Her Ladyship" Marisa said to Jim, "I want her to have plenty of exercise so you need not be back here until noon."

"Very good, Miss!" Jim answered and then he said to Aline: "We'll start off down the gallop, M'Lady, Firefly be rather frisky this morning."

"I will race you," Aline replied.

"Very good, M'Lady," Jim replied, "how big a start do you want?"

They were chattering cheerfully as they rode away down the drive.

Aline turned once to wave and Marisa waved back forcing away a lump in her throat before she said to the Butler standing beside her:

"I have to catch a train to London this morning, Turner. Will you please order a carriage to be round in about half an hour."

"Going to London, Miss!" Turner exclaimed in surprise.

"Unfortunately" Marisa answered. "But I have not told her Ladyship as I thought she might be upset. I will leave a note for her upstairs explaining that I have been called away."

"Very good, Miss."

Marisa went upstairs. As she reached the second floor she could see through the open door of her bed-room three housemaids packing her clothes in the big round-topped leather trunks that Lady Berrington had given her.

She wanted to cry out at the sight, to find some excuse, some reason why she could stay.

Then she remembered that she must be gone not only by the time Aline returned, but before the Duke came back from shooting.

She had been half afraid when she rose that he was somewhere in the Castle, but fortunately without her having to ask the question as to where he might be, Aline had asked it for her.

"His Grace came back unexpectedly last night" Nanny had announced when she had come into the School-Room.

She had been, as Aline anticipated, extremely jealous to find that Marisa had usurped one of her privileges and dressed Aline, but she could not resist imparting a piece of information about the Duke.

"I thought Papa was away" Aline said, "I am riding with him tomorrow!"

"Well he's back" Nanny had said in an uncompromising voice, "so perhaps His Grace will wish for you to go riding with him today—alone."

She accentuated the last word and looked at Marisa spitefully. Aline had told everyone that she was riding with her father on Wednesday.

Nanny obviously had no idea that Marisa had been asked to accompany them.

"Oh do you think Papa will take me with him today as well, Miss Mitton?" Aline asked eagerly.

Before Marisa could reply, Gladys who was helping one of the footmen to serve the breakfast answered:

"His Grace has gone shooting, Miss Aline. I heard Mr. Turner say in the pantry that His Grace 'd accepted another invitation and had been up extra early because he'd a long way to go."

"Then I cannot ride with him today, can I?" Aline said with an unanswerable logic.

If the Duke was shooting some distance away, Marisa thought, he would not be back until six o'clock at least, or later.

As far as he was concerned, there was plenty of time for her to leave the Castle, but at the same time she had no desire to upset Aline and that meant she must depart at the first possible moment.

She wrote the child an affectionate note saying she had been called away unexpectedly.

Then she put it in an envelope, addressed it to Aline and laid it on the School-Room table.

She went into her own bed-room. Despite the services of three housemaids there still seemed quite a lot of things waiting to be packed into the trunks.

"Just push the clothes in any way" she said.

"Oh no, Miss!" Gladys protested, "you wouldn't want these lovely gowns to be crushed."

Marisa realised there was no chance of hurrying the maids, so she went downstairs and along the corridor to Miss Whitcham's office. Miss Whitcham had the Chef with her and they were working out the menu for dinner.

She looked up in surprise as Marisa entered.

"Good morning, Miss Mitton" she said and then to the Chef, "that will be all, Chef. If you cannot get the quails that His Grace likes so much, you will have to change the dish to partridges."

"Very good, Miss Whitcham," the Chef said and bowing to Marisa went from the room.

"I thought you had gone riding with Aline," Miss Whitcham said in surprise.

"I did not go with her this morning" Marisa answered, "because I have had an urgent message which necessitates my leaving for London."

"Leaving!" Miss Whitcham exclaimed, "I hope it is not bad news."

"I am afraid it is," Marisa said quietly. "I have not told Aline that I have to go, but I have left a note for her upstairs."

"Oh dear this is troublesome!" Miss Whitcham said, "what shall I say to His Grace? He will be most distressed to hear that you have to go away just as Aline is getting on so well with her lessons. And apart from her lapse where Lady Wantage was concerned, she is so much better behaved than she has ever been before."

"I am glad you should think so" Marisa said. "She is a dear little girl. I have suggested to the Duke that she would benefit considerably if she could have lessons with other children. There must be some little girls, or even little boys on the Estate and the one governess could teach them all. It would engender a sense of competition which I think is important where children are concerned."

"What did His Grace say to such an idea?" Miss Whitcham exclaimed in surprise.

"He said he would think about it," Marisa answered. "Do encourage him Miss Whitcham, to agree! It really would be so good for Aline."

"You must encourage His Grace yourself," Miss Whitcham replied. "After all you will not be gone for long."

"I hope not" Marisa answered. "But if I am, please find Aline a young sympathetic governess. She is very easy to teach if she is interested."

"You're the only one who has ever said so," Miss Whitcham retorted. "But do not let us talk of finding anyone else. You will be back, of course you will be back! Is it your father or mother who is ill?"

"Neither," Marisa replied, "but I have to leave and I think my things are nearly ready."

She held out her hand to Miss Whitcham as she spoke.

"Goodbye and thank you for being so kind to me."

"Oh my dear you have nothing for which to thank me" Miss Whitcham replied genially, "it has been a real pleasure to have you with me. It's a long time since I've had someone to talk to, someone who seemed to understand. I'm often very lonely, you know."

"I am sure you are," Marisa answered and hurried from the room in case Miss Whitcham should ask more questions.

Finally her trunks were carried downstairs and Marisa followed them wearing the blue travelling gown and mantle in which she had come to Vox.

When she looked at herself in the mirror she realised she looked smart, elegant and extremely pretty.

"It is extraordinary" she thought, "that the agony I am suffering does not show on my face."

When she reached the front door she found there was a closed Brougham to take her to the station and behind it a luggage cart, both drawn by two well-bred horses.

"Goodbye, Turner," Marisa said to the Butler.

"Goodbye, Miss, I hope you have a pleasant journey. The footmen will signal the train and see that your trunks are taken safely aboard."

"Thank you very much," Marisa said.

This was the last time, she thought, that she would drive in the Duke's carriage, attended to by his servants, the last time she would enjoy such luxury, such grandeur.

But she knew that most of all she would miss the beauty of the Castle.

In the October sunshine, the lakes were molten silver and the leaves falling from the great trees in the Park were gold and russet red.

A flight of white pigeons winged their way swiftly across the sky, and a grey heron flapped slowly above the rushes.

Marisa knew behind her the Norman tower, its stone walls mellowed with age, stood sentinel over the gabled roofs with their elegant Georgian towers. Its arrow slits were in strange contrast to the long wide paned windows built in the reign of Queen Anne.

Vox Castle—the voice of the Norman who had built it! A place where she had found love and lost it.

A love from which, she knew, she would never be free for the rest of her life.

Marisa moved down the steps towards the brougham when she saw Turner who was beside her glance in surprise over her head towards the Park. Instinctively she looked too.

Urging his horse forward and galloping towards them at great speed was a man on a horse.

For one second Marisa did not recognise him and then she saw it was Jim and he was alone.

"Surely that is Jim" she said quickly.

"It is, Miss" Turner replied.

"Perhaps there has been an accident!" Marisa exclaimed. "What could have happened to Her Ladyship?"

Agitated she started to walk down the drive towards the oncoming horseman.

As Jim saw her he reined in his mount who was sweating from the speed at which he had been ridden, and flung himself from the saddle.

"Miss Mitton! It's her Ladyship" he said his voice breathless.

"What has happened?" Marisa asked.

"They've taken her away, Miss, they've kidnapped her! There were nothin' I could do."

"What do you mean?" Marisa enquired bewildered.

"The strikers, Miss, six of 'em. Three of 'em on horses, if you'd call such animals a horse. They took hold of her Ladyship's reins and tells I to come back here with a note for His Grace. She crys out to me not to leave her, Miss, but there was nothin' I could do and I thinks it best to come home as they said."

Marisa drew a deep breath.

"Give me the note," she managed to say in a voice which shook.

Jim pulled a dirty piece of paper from his pocket. It was not sealed and Marisa opened it.

The words were written in capitals in an uneducated hand, scrawled across the paper and mis-spelt.

"US HAVE TAKIN YER LITTLE GAL. HER CAN BE COLD AND HUNGERY LIKE ORES BE UNLESS YE AGRES TER WHAT WE ASKS OF YE."

Marisa stared at the note trying to take in the sense of it. Then she said in a voice which sounded strangely unlike her own.

"You said 'the strikers'. What strikers?"

"The men at the iron-mine, Miss. They've been on strike this past three weeks. They're rough and I only hopes they won't hurt her Ladyship."

Marisa turned and walked back to the steps where Turner was still waiting beside the carriage.

"Where is His Grace?" she asked.

"He's shooting with Colonel Fitzgerald, Miss. When Lord Acton was taken ill yesterday, the Colonel invited the guests to shoot on his Estate. His Grace left at eight o'clock this morning."

"He must be asked to return immediately" Marisa said, "how long will it take to reach him?"

"It would take a groom riding across country a good hour, Miss, and it would take His Grace about an hour and a half to drive back with his four in hand. Is there something wrong with Her Ladyship?"

"Something very wrong" Marisa replied. "His Grace must be notified at once. I will write a note. Get a groom round from the stable."

Turner looked for a moment as if he was surprised at her for giving orders. Then he said:

"I'll do that immediately, Miss."

Marisa turned to enter the house then she hesitated.

"I also want a horse and a groom to come with me" she said. "Get Gladys downstairs to tell you which of these trunks contains my riding-habit."

"Very good, Miss" Turner said.

Then as if he could not repress his curiosity he asked:

"What has happened to her Ladyship?"

"Jim will tell you what has occurred" Marisa replied and passing across the Hall walked quickly towards the Library.

There was writing-paper and a pen and ink on the big desk in the centre of the room. Just for a moment she remembered what had happened last night when the Duke had read her manuscript.

Then she dismissed the thought from her mind and concentrated only on Aline.

The child would be frightened, there would be no doubt about that. If only, Marisa thought, she had been with her.

But how could anyone have anticipated anything so unusual and so unexpected could have happened at Vox?

She had heard of gypsies kidnapping children and selling them to beggars, but never had she imagined that strikers in any industry might do such a thing.

Then in horror, she wondered what the Duke would say. He had trusted her to look after Aline and she had failed him! Would he hold her responsible?

Even if he did, it was of no consequence. All that mattered was Aline—afraid and alone!

Marisa had seen her abductors last week when she and Aline had ridden by the mine and spoken to three of the miners. She remembered now that one of them had asked if Aline was the Duke's little girl.

It must have been their seeing the child that had put

the idea into their minds to kidnap her and force the Duke to agree to their demands.

"It is my fault!" Marisa thought with a stabbing anxiety which made her want to cry out frantically at the thought of Aline being in the power of such men.

Then she knew that she must keep her head. It was no use waiting for the Duke.

It would be two or three hours before he could return to the Castle and in the meantime Aline must not be left alone and terrified.

Hastily Marisa scribbled a note.

"Aline has been kidnapped. Please return immediately."
                                        Marisa Mitton

She folded the thick white paper with the ducal crest on it and placed it in the envelope.

She addressed it to "His Grace the Duke of Milverley" and hurrying from the Library gave it to Turner who was waiting in the Hall.

"Send this at once to His Grace" Marisa said.

"A groom is waiting, Miss" Turner replied, "and Gladys has identified the trunk which contains your habit, Miss. A footman has taken it upstairs to your bed-room."

"Good! See that a horse is here by the time I have changed."

Marisa spoke in a tone of authority that she had not used since she came to Vox, and without waiting for Turner's answer she ran up the Grand Staircase and up the next flight to her bed-room.

It took her less than five minutes to change and she came running down again to find the horse she habitually rode was outside the front door. Beside it mounted on another superb piece of horse flesh was Hanson.

She knew by the expressions on the faces of the servants seeing her off, that they were all deeply perturbed but she was not prepared to discuss it.

Only as she was helped into the saddle did Turner say in a low voice:

"The groom has left for His Grace, Miss. We are all hoping you will not find her Ladyship in any distress."

"I hope so too" Marisa replied.

As her horse was frisky Marisa, followed by Hanson, galloped across the park and only when they reached the woods and were forced to go slowly did she speak to him.

"Why are the iron-miners on strike?" she asked.

"They say the mine isn't safe, Miss" the Head Groom answered. "A man got crushed by a fall of stone caused by faulty pit-props nearly a month ago."

"Did he die?"

"Yes, Miss. But Mr. Nicholson, I understands, would give his family no compensation."

"Who is Mr. Nicholson?"

"His Grace's Agent, Miss. He runs the Estate and has always been against the iron-miners. He's wanted to shut the mine for years, but His Grace wouldn't hear of it."

"Why not?"

"Well His Grace said the mine had been worked in his father's time and his grandfather's, and if he turned the miners off they were not trained for any other type of work. It would mean they would starve or go on the Parish."

"What sort of men are they?" Marisa enquired.

"Rough, Miss, they ain't had a chance to be anything else."

Hanson was silent for a moment and then he added:

"My grandfather when he was a lad used to work in one of the iron pits on the Estate. They were considered essential in those days."

"There were a lot of them in this country, I believe" Marisa said.

"That's true, Miss. But they used to burn wood in the kilns then and it was said this meant cutting down too many trees. So most of the pits were closed."

"But His Grace's pit uses coal. I saw a stack of it the other day while we were riding past the mine."

Hanson glanced at Marisa for a moment as if he would have commented at her being near the iron-pit. Then he said:

"It's His Grace's father who had the coal brought to the mine. He built a track to carry it from the highway and the miners push the trucks on rails right up to the pit."

"There seemed quite a number of men working there," Marisa said.

"About thirty or forty, Miss."

"Is that not rather a lot?"

"It's quite a big pit, Miss. Goes back a long way, but Mr. Nicholson has spent nothing on it for years and the props are worn. Some crumble in the damp and the men have often complained that he will not give them the proper tools."

"What happens now they are on strike?" Marisa asked.

"They goes hungry, Miss," Hanson replied grimly.

They were through the wood by now and Marisa spurred on her horse. She had no time for further conversation but concentrated on getting to the mine as quickly as possible.

Only when she came in sight of it did she rein in her horse in the shadows of some trees and say:

"I want you to stay here, Hanson."

"You're not there going alone, Miss!"

"I shall be much safer alone than with you," Marisa declared. "I am going to talk to the men and if they will not let me return to report what is happening to the Duke, then I will stay with her Ladyship."

She looked towards the mine and added:

"Wait for an hour and a half, and if I have not come back by then return to the Castle and tell the Duke what has happened."

"I'll do that, Miss—but be careful."

"I will try to be," Marisa answered.

She cantered away leaving the groom looking after her with a worried expression on his face.

She must have been seen long before she arrived, because as she finally drew up to the front of the mine there were at least twenty men waiting to receive her.

She pulled her horse to a standstill, noting with a sinking of her heart that they looked both rough and aggressive and that many of them held thick sticks or cudgels in their hands.

"I am Miss Mitton, her Ladyship's governess," Marisa said quietly in her soft voice. "I have come to see if I can help—and I mean help."

"What can ye do?" an elderly man asked harshly.

"Aye, what can ye do?" several others repeated in a kind of ugly chorus.

"Well, first of all you can tell me if Lady Aline is safe and not frightened," Marisa said. "She is only a child, and while you gentlemen are entitled to argue over your difficulties, there can be no possible reason for her to suffer unnecessarily."

"Our children be a suffering," one of the men said, "there ain't been nowt to eat these last three days."

"That's true, that's true enough," a number of the others agreed.

"Then the sooner we settle this matter the better," Marisa replied.

"Aye, and we'll settle it on our terms," the older man who had spoken first said, "or else th' Dook's daughter 'll have a taste of what our kids have had ter put up with."

"Take me to her," Marisa said insistently, "and then I want you to tell me exactly what your terms are. I understand the mine is not safe."

"T'be dangerous in many places," the older man said, "and if th' Dook comes after us with th' police or th' military we'll put his gal still further inside."

"She is not in the mine now!" Marisa exclaimed with horror. "She is frightened of the dark."

"That's th' place for her then" a man answered.

"Help me dismount," Marisa said abruptly.

For a moment she thought the men might refuse, and then several hands went out to help her alight. On the ground she felt afraid because they were so much taller than she was.

Then she looked up into the face of the older man and said quietly:

"Take me to Lady Aline so that I can see you have not harmed her. After that we will discuss what can be done to help you. The Duke is away from home. I have sent for him, but he cannot be at the Castle for nearly three hours."

"Be that th' truth?" the man asked.

"It is the truth, I promise you," Marisa replied.

He looked at her sharply to see if she might be lying. Satisfied he said roughly.

"Come along with Oi' ".

There were some half-hearted protests from the other men, but taking no notice of them he led Marisa to the edge of the mine and then as she picked up her skirts, they entered into the darkness.

There was a candle-lantern hanging on the wall.

The man took it in his hand and they started down a dark airless tunnel, Marisa following him had to bend her head because her high-crowned hat made it impossible for her to stand upright.

There was a smell of earth and burnt coal. A smell too of sweat and something else which Marisa thought was fear.

She wondered if the sides of the passage might cave in and crush her or the jagged roof collapse on her head.

She wondered what it would be to work in such an atmosphere year after year. It would be bad enough without wondering day after day if one would come out alive.

Finally when she began to wonder if in fact she was being taken to Aline or to some sort of prison in which she would be incarcerated, the tunnel widened out and there by the light of another lantern, Marisa could see a small opening.

In it Aline was sitting on the wooden box and near her also sitting down was a man.

Aline, giving a shrill cry of joy at the sight of Marisa, jumped to her feet and ran towards her.

"Oh you have come! You have come!" she cried, "I was so frightened that you would never find me."

She burst into tears as she spoke. Marisa knelt down and put her arms round her, holding her close.

"It is all right, darling," she said soothingly, "I am here!"

The man who had been sitting beside Aline got slowly to his feet.

"Her be all right" he said in a surly tone, "her ain't come ter no harm."

"No, of course not," Marisa agreed, "but she is afraid of the dark. It was kind of you to be with her."

"Oi were a stopping her from running away," the man said. "Hers tried it several times."

"I tried to ... escape" Aline muttered through her sobs, "but he ... caught me."

"Never mind, darling," Marisa replied, "I am sure these

gentlemen will let you come out now while they tell me what this is all about."

She looked at the older man as she spoke.

"Can we do that please?"

He looked uncomfortable and could not meet her eyes.

"She is only nine," Marisa said softly, "let us talk outside."

"Oi suppose we can" he said grudgingly, "but ye b'ain't taking her home. We're keeping her here 'til th' Dook gives we our rights."

"Oh make Papa do that! Make him" Aline said in an urgent whisper.

"I am sure the Duke will agree to your requests if they are reasonable," Marisa said.

"They be reasonable enough," both men tried to say at once.

"I have the feeling" Marisa went on, "that His Grace has no idea of your difficulties. He may not even know you are on strike."

"Mr. Nicholson knows right enough," the older man said.

"Mr. Nicholson is not the Duke," Marisa replied, "and you know as well as I do that when messages are passed from one person to another, it is easy to get a distorted picture of what is happening."

She rose to her feet as she spoke taking her arms from Aline but holding her by the hand.

"Now can we go outside in the sunshine? I hate this gloomy place as much as this little girl does."

"We've ter put up with it," the man said who had been sitting with Aline.

"But I do not suppose you often bring your children here" Marisa retorted and he did not reply.

Slowly they progressed back the way Marisa had come.

Then as they came out into the sunshine Aline rubbed her eyes, streaking her face from her dirty hands as she did so.

The men surrounding the entrance were glaring at them.

"Now where can we sit down and talk?" Marisa asked pleasantly as if she was at an ordinary tea party. "I think it would be much more comfortable than standing?"

She walked as she spoke through the ranks of the men and past the slag heaps and the debris which littered the front of the mine. Finally she reached a hillock where the grass looked fairly clean.

She sat down on it drawing Aline down beside her. The men obviously non-plussed by her attitude stood round in a circle, partly, Marisa knew, to prevent her making any attempt to escape.

"Please sit," she pleaded. "You are all so tall it rather overwhelms me."

In a surly manner they obeyed her. Then as she handed Aline her handkerchief to wipe her face she said conversationally:

"Now tell me exactly what you want."

They all tried to talk at once until finally Marisa insisted on hearing the older man first. It was obvious as she listened they had a very genuine grievance.

It took time to hear it all.

As Hanson had said, no modernisation had been carried out in the mine for a long time, no money had been spent on it, safety precautions were non-existent.

The man who had died from being crushed to death following the collapse of the props had left a wife and five children. They had only managed to survive by the others making a contribution every week out of their very small wage.

It was obvious the men had gone on strike in a fit of rebellion and Marisa guessed that because Mr. Nicholson disliked the men and because he thought he would bring them to his knees, he had just left them alone.

Their work was not essential, the fact there was no iron ore coming from the mine had apparently worried no-one, and in a desperate attempt not to surrender, they were slowly starving themselves.

They had managed to snare a few rabbits, they had eaten all the hens which provided them with eggs before the strike, and finally they had become desperate.

After Marisa and Aline's visit, some of the younger men had thought of kidnapping the child in a last effort to gain the attention of the Duke.

It was the younger ones who spoke the most ferociously.

"If he won't give us what we asks, we'll take that little gal into th' mine and put here where no-one 'll find her. If she screams herself ter death it won't be our business."

The youth who said this spoke so fiercely that Aline trembled with fear and turned towards Marisa and hid her face against her shoulder.

"Nonsense!" Marisa said with a smile, "you are all of you far too good natured to do anything so cruel. What I am going to suggest is this. I will ride back to the Castle and tell the Duke as soon as he returns what you have told me. Then I will bring him here to see the mine and to discuss the trouble with you."

"More likely he'll send Nicholson with the police," one of the men said.

"I promise you he will not do that," Marisa replied, "I can only beg of you to trust me."

"Ye 're not a taking her with ye," one of the men said jerking a thumb towards Aline.

"No of course not!" Marisa agreed, "I quite understand that you want to keep her as a hostage."

"Take me! Take me!" Aline cried.

"Now listen, Aline," Marisa said in a voice that everyone could hear, "you are the representative of your father and of the Estate. These men have a grievance with which I am very sympathetic and I think your father will be sympathetic too."

She held the child close to her as she continued.

"I am sure he has not been told the true facts of their case, he may not even have been told how much they have suffered or that one man has died because the mine has been neglected. I am going to bring him back here to see for himself what is going on."

"I want to . . . come with . . . you," Aline pleaded pathetically.

"You cannot do that," Marisa replied, "because these gentlemen are afraid that we might gallop away and never come back. But what I am going to suggest, Aline, is that they take you into one of their houses. I am sure there you will find a little girl of your own age."

She smiled at Aline.

"I want you to talk to her and tell her about all those toys we put on one side, and then if she would like to have them you can bring them to her one day in your pony-cart."

"I do not want to . . . stay here without . . . you," Aline murmured.

"And let your Papa think you are a coward?" Marisa enquired.

"Would . . . Papa . . . want me to . . . stay?" Aline asked.

"Of course he would, because you are representing him," Marisa answered. "I shall not be long. I will ride home, wait for your father and we will both be back as soon as possible. But first of all I am going to ask these gentlemen to show me where you can stay while I am gone."

She rose to her feet as she spoke and the men rose too.

"Oi suppose it be all right," one of them said doubtfully, "if we have th' child, he won't bring no guns against us."

"Of course he will not" Marisa said. "I promise you that! I promise you too I will bring the Duke alone. There will be nobody with him—no police, no guards, no grooms, just the Duke alone with me. Is that fair?"

"If he comes" one man said doubtfully, but it was obvious the others had accepted Marisa's proposition.

"Now come along and show me where Lady Aline can wait" she said. "Which of you has a little girl of nine?"

"Oi have" one man replied, "and five other brats as well."

"Well, let us go and meet them," Marisa smiled.

They walked slowly in a group across the rough grass towards the houses.

Some looked particularly dirty and unkempt and Marisa was relieved to see that the one to which she was being taken by the father of the child of nine looked a little more prepossessing. It even had a number of panes of glass in its windows.

There were women and children standing in the doorways of the houses they passed and several dogs lying outside.

It struck Marisa they were all unnaturally quiet. The children should have been shouting and playing, the dogs barking. One did raise his head and give a feeble yap but he did it lying down.

Then with a kind of sick horror Marisa understood!

They were all—women, children and dogs—weak for want of food. The truth was clear to see in their pale faces and tired lack-lustre eyes.

They were emaciated to the point when it was too much effort even to cry.

The inside of the house was horrifying.

There was a small fire in the grate burning logs which had obviously been collected from the surrounding woods. The walls were black with smoke, the plaster broken away.

There was a bare deal table, three broken chairs and on the floor old mattresses which would not bear inspection covered with threadbare blankets and pieces of rag.

A woman who was sitting by the fire was suckling a baby. Marisa noted with relief that she had a kind face.

There were two little girls in the room besides two younger children, one of Aline's age and another perhaps eighteen months older. They were bare-footed and although their clothes were ragged they were comparatively clean.

They all stared open mouthed as Marisa holding Aline by the hand came into the room.

The man explained to his wife briefly that Aline was to stay with her and not to escape until the Duke was brought to the mine.

The woman took the baby from her breast and rose to her feet.

"We aint got no comforts here, M'am" she said to Marisa.

"I can see that," Marisa answered.

"Th' children be hungry, they've had nowt but a few taties" the woman murmured, "some of the men are out searching for what they can find."

"Stealing it'll be called if they be caught" her husband said harshly.

"What is your name?" Marisa asked the woman.

"Crake, M'am."

"I would be most grateful Mrs. Crake if you would look after Lady Aline, while I return to the Castle."

"Oi'll do me best" Mrs. Crake replied, but she looked doubtful.

"I will see what I can arrange about some food for all the children" Marisa promised.

She bent down to Aline.

"Stay with these little girls and I promise you I will bring your Papa back as quickly as I can. Remember I want you to be brave and show everyone here your pretty manners."

Aline's eyes were suddenly full of tears. She did not say anything, but merely put her arms round Marisa's neck and hugged her.

"I am proud of you," Marisa said softly.

Then rising to her feet she said to the father of the children.

"Now if I can have my horse I will go back to the Castle and fetch the Duke."

She went outside to find the horse was waiting for her.

The other men were staring at her curiously and there was still a great deal of suspicion in their eyes, but they helped her mount.

Then as she rode away, one said with something like a grudging admiration:

"Good luck, M'am."

"That is what I hope to bring you" Marisa replied and galloped off.

Chapter Eight

Marisa arrived back at the Castle to find half the household waiting in the Hall, and as she dismounted Miss Whitcham came hurrying down the steps.

"Is Aline all right?" she asked frantically. "Tell me quickly what has happened?"

"Aline will be quite all right" Marisa replied and then from Turner who was waiting at the top of the steps she enquired:

"What is the time?"

"It is nearly half after one, Miss," Turner replied. "His Grace by this time should be on his way home."

"I hope so," Marisa murmured.

"Of course, Miss," Turner continued, "we have to allow for the extra time it might take to find the shooting-party. If they are some way from the house across the fields, it would not be possible for His Grace to drive back the moment the groom reached him."

"No, of course not," Marisa agreed.

She looked round at the anxious faces of the Housekeeper, the housemaids, the footmen, the Duke's valets, the Chef and a large number of other servants whom she could not identify.

"Lady Aline is quite safe," she said raising her voice a little, "and as soon as His Grace returns I have promised that he will visit the mine and listen to the grievances of the men."

There was an expression of relief on the faces of those listening.

"In the meantime," Marisa said to Turner, "I want one of the open brakes to carry all the food that can be spared from the kitchens to the families of the miners."

"Oh really, Miss Mitton," Miss Whitcham interposed, "I don't think we can do that! We must wait for His Grace or at least inform Mr. Nicholson. He'd want to know what is happening, and I'm sure he would think it most odd."

"I am not concerned with what Mr. Nicholson thinks one way or another," Marisa said coldly, "and I take full responsibility for seeing the food reaches the women and children as quickly as possible."

She paused to think and went on—

"There will be a great number of hams in the kitchens; I am sure there will be rabbits and hares amongst the game that was shot on Saturday. All the bread that is in the Castle is to be put in the shooting-brake; the cooks can bake more for the household."

She saw the incredulous expression on Miss Whitcham's face and added, putting her hand on her arm:

"I assure you, the matter is urgent and concerns Aline's safety."

She had known that these were magic words which would turn the tide in her favour. Instantly Miss Whitcham was cooperative.

"I will go to the kitchens myself," she said, "you will want eggs of course."

"And all the butter that can be spared," Marisa said.

Miss Whitcham hurried away, and Marisa said to Turner:

"Send two grooms with the brake besides a coachman, and please arrange that sharp carving knives are sent with the meat. I intend to cut up the food and distribute it amongst the families."

"How many people are you catering for, Miss?" Turner asked.

If Marisa had not been so worried she would have smiled at his tone, because he spoke as if she were arranging a social soirèe.

"I think there must be about fifty adults" she replied, "and perhaps nearly thirty children. It is difficult to judge, but certainly they are hungry."

She had planned what she would ask for on her way back to the Castle and now she remembered something else.

"One thing more, Turner. Send a man to the Home Farm. They should be starting the afternoon milking very shortly. Instruct them that all the milk is to be sent immediately to the mine. They can also include more eggs on the cart and butter."

"I will see it is attended to immediately, Miss," Turner replied.

He started to give one of the footmen instructions to run to the stable and order the brake.

"Hanson will be outside," Marisa interrupted remembering the groom had come back with her from the mine.

"I will speak to him myself," Turner said.

"And one more thing," Marisa continued, "as soon as His Grace appears, tell the grooms to bring Samson round and also a fresh horse for me."

Turner walked with dignity down the front steps to speak to the Head Groom and Marisa hurried up the stairs thinking she would have time to wash her hands before the Duke arrived.

"Can't I get you something, Miss Mitton?" the House-keeper asked as she passed her, "you've missed your lunch."

"Thank you but I could not eat anything," Marisa replied.

"What about a cup of tea?" the House-keeper suggested.

"That would be very nice," Marisa answered, "but I would like it down here. I want to be waiting when His Grace arrives."

She only spent a few minutes in her room washing her hands and tidying herself, then going into the School Room she took from the table the letter which she had left for Aline.

She put it in a drawer in her bed-room and hoped that no-one would be so stupid as to mention to Aline that all her boxes had been packed and were downstairs.

Then feeling that these matters were of minor importance, Marisa hurried down again into the Hall.

A cup of tea was waiting for her and while she was drinking it, Miss Whitcham came back from the kitchens.

"We have collected enough food to feed a regiment of soldiers!" she answered.

"I hope it is enough for a lot of very hungry miners and their families," Marisa replied.

"I'm sure I don't know what His Grace will say," Miss Whitcham went on, shaking her head, "and as for Mr. Nicholson!"

"I have told you that I will take full responsibility," Marisa said and her voice was hard.

What did it matter, she thought to herself, if the Duke was annoyed or if Mr. Nicholson was ranting with rage?

Riding back from the mine she had felt a surge of anger against the Duke.

She remembered the enormous amount of food that had been consumed the past weekend when the Prince of Wales was present, the exotic dishes that had succeeded each other at the dinner on Thursday night at which she had been present.

Quails, ortolans, pâté de foie gras, truffles and caviar had been served besides every other possible luxury that the mind could imagine.

Yet only a few miles away the miners' children had been crying themselves to sleep because they were hungry.

No wonder, Marisa thought, her father had denounced Society as unfeeling and irresponsible.

But, because she loved the Duke, she could not help praying he had not been aware of what was happening on his Estate.

She was sure that Mr. Nicholson had not proposed to him that they should starve them out and that he had acquiesced.

She was sure that when he saw the white, thin faces of the children, he would realise that something had to be done and quickly.

Nevertheless she was honest enough to admit to herself that the reason she was in such a hurry to get the food away from the Castle was that she was not entirely confident that the Duke, once he knew of such a project, would permit it.

He might want to delay, to talk first and act afterwards, and that was what Marisa was determined to prevent.

"Has the brake left?" she asked Miss Whitcham.

"If not, it will do so at any moment," Miss Whitcham replied. "The Chef and the other cooks entered into the spirit of the thing—it was an unexpected excitement! There's not a crumb of bread left in the Castle and they are quite happy to start baking again, even so late in the day!"

"I hope there is enough," Marisa murmured almost to herself.

"I am sure there will be," Miss Whitcham assured her. "There was half a stag in the game-larder, so I told them to send that too."

Marisa smiled at her.

"Thank you, I felt that when you knew how much was at stake, you would not fail me."

"I was thinking of Aline," Miss Whitcham answered. "I am sure she is terribly frightened being left with those wicked men."

"They are not wicked," Marisa replied, "they are rough and uneducated and I think too they are bewildered to find how unimportant they are. They are also at the moment a little afraid of their own courage."

Miss Whitcham did not understand and Marisa knew that she was only formulating her own thoughts. She was well aware that the miners had treated her with a respect and a gentleness which under other circumstances might not have been in evidence.

They were not wicked men, but desperate ones.

They had tried to draw attention to themselves and their suffering by the only means they knew but they were no match for the cleverness of Mr. Nicholson who had defeated them by sheer indifference.

"Please God make the Duke understand and help them" Marisa prayed in her heart.

It seemed that time had never gone so slowly. She kept looking at the grandfather clock which stood in one corner of the Hall.

She looked at it so often that she felt as though the hands were not moving and the clock must have stopped, but it was only her own impatience for the Duke's arrival.

A quarter to two—two o'clock came and still there was no sign of him.

Finally it was nearly twenty past the hour before one of the footmen standing at the Hall door exclaimed:

"Here he comes!"

Marisa moved forward quickly. She saw at the far end of the drive four horses proceeding through the park, the sunshine glittering on their silver harness.

There was a cloud of dust behind the vehicle which told her that the Duke was travelling swiftly. Then suddenly for the first time, her defiance seemed to ebb away from her and she felt nervous.

"When His Grace arrives, I wish to speak to him alone," she said to Turner in a low voice, "please ask him to come immediately to the Study."

"Very good, Miss," Turner replied.

Marisa looked at Miss Whitcham.

"I think it would be best for me to tell His Grace exactly what has occurred" she said.

Miss Whitcham took the hint.

"I will go upstairs. But, oh dear, I feel sure His Grace will expect us to have done more to try and save Aline!"

Marisa did not reply, she merely walked across the Hall and down the corridor to the Duke's Study.

She left the door ajar and moved across the room to the window. She suddenly felt very cold.

She had not expected to see the Duke again.

She had thought this morning when she rose and dressed that it was very unlikely she would ever in her whole life set eyes on him even at a distance, and it would of course be unconceivable for them ever to meet.

"Damn you, get out of my sight!" he had said last night and she had tried to obey him.

But circumstances had been too strong for her and now she was waiting for him, waiting with a kind of sick fear that was a physical pain within her breast.

She had heard the murmur of voices in the Hall, and yet when he actually entered the room it came almost as a shock.

He stood there large, tall, broad shouldered, and Marisa knew by the way he was frowning that he was extremely incensed.

"What has happened, Miss Mitton?" he asked harshly. "Your note told me Aline has been kidnapped and the groom informs me it is by the iron-miners."

"That is right," Marisa answered, "they were waiting for Aline when she went riding this morning and they sent the groom who accompanied her back to the Castle with a note for you. I have it here."

She drew a piece of paper as she spoke from the pocket of her habit and held it out towards him. The Duke made no effort to take it.

"Why were you not with Aline?" he enquired, and it seemed to her that there was an accusative tone in his voice.

"I had a ... headache," Marisa answered feeling she could not tell him the truth at that moment.

She dropped her eyes as she spoke and the Duke moved forward to take the note from her. He read it and then threw it down on the desk.

"Damn it!" he exclaimed. "Why was I not told they were on strike?"

"You did not know?"

"Nicholson mentioned they were dissatisfied," he answered, "but I did not realise it was anything serious."

He turned as he spoke and moved towards the door.

"Where are you going?" Marisa asked.

"To get my own men together and send a groom for the police."

"Please, you must not do that," Marisa pleaded. "I have promised the miners that you will come to the mine alone, that you will listen to their grievances, and that you will not be accompanied by anyone but me."

The Duke turned round with an expression of almost stupefaction on his face.

"You promised who?" he asked.

"The miners!"

"You say you have promised them—how?"

"I have been to the mine," Marisa replied, "I have talked with the miners."

"You went—alone?"

"Hanson waited for me in the woods. I went alone because it was the only way I could see Aline and rescue her. They had hidden her inside the mine."

"Inside the mine!"

The Duke's voice was almost an explosion.

"How dare they! I will shoot every one of them for doing such a thing!"

"She is not there now," Marisa explained. "I brought her

out and she is waiting in one of their houses with a child of her own age. She is no longer frightened and she realises she is a hostage."

"You have arranged all this!" the Duke exclaimed. "I cannot understand what has happened or what part you have played in the matter. It sounds to me completely and utterly insane!"

He spoke so angrily that Marisa felt her own temper rise.

"The men have a genuine grievance" she said. "You may not have been told what is going on on your Estate, and I am giving you credit for not realising how very serious the situation is. The pit is unsafe, but your Agent would not listen to the miners' complaints, not even when a man was killed from a fall of stone because the pit-props have rotted."

She saw the anger fade from the Duke's face.

"Is this true?"

"I have seen the condition of the mine for myself," Marisa said, "and I have promised that you will see it too."

"You expect me to go there alone?" the Duke asked.

"They will not hurt you," Marisa replied scornfully, "not if you try to understand what they are suffering. And quite frankly you have no alternative but to come and see the conditions in which they are working as I have promised you will do."

"And to make sure I do what you wanted, you left Aline as a hostage?" the Duke said.

"What do you expect me to have done about it once they had captured her?" Marisa enquired crossly. "Fight twenty men single-handed in an effort to rescue her? And if you take the police against them, which is what they originally expected you to do, then it is very doubtful if, when the battle is over, you will find Aline alive."

There was silence as Marisa stopped speaking.

"I understand that you have done what you thought was best," the Duke said at length in a very different tone of voice. "I will go and change my clothes. Will you order a horse for me?"

"I have already done so," Marisa answered. "And one

thing more—I have sent all the food that is available in the Castle to the mine."

"You have done what?"

Again the Duke seemed utterly astonished.

"They have been on strike for three weeks," Marisa said, "they have no money and they have nothing left to eat."

"Surely you could have waited until I have spoken with the men."

He did not sound angry, but there was a rebuke in his voice which Marisa resented.

"The children are suffering," she said. "Do you not understand? They are starving! Even a few hours in their life will seem a long time."

She felt that he was still critical and her chin went up.

"I told Miss Whitcham I would take full responsibility for sending the food," she said. "If you feel it was an unnecessary extravagance I am quite prepared to pay for it out of my own pocket."

There was a sudden flash of anger in the Duke's eyes.

"And how, Miss Mitton, could you afford to do that?" he asked. "Or are you perhaps offering to reimburse me with the proceeds from the sale of your book?"

His words were like the stroke of a whip.

For a moment Marisa went even paler than she was already and then the blood flared into her cheeks.

"I am sorry, forgive me," the Duke said in a very different tone of voice before she could speak, "I should not have said that. I apologise."

Marisa could not answer him, but questioningly she looked up into his face. Their eyes met, and for a moment they were both very still.

Then the Duke turned away and without a word went upstairs to change his clothes.

It was not long before they were riding swiftly across the park. At first Marisa's new horse was frisky and she had difficulty in keeping it under control.

There was however nothing that she wished to say to the Duke, and she was conscious that he was looking stern and grim, his chin square, his lips set in a hard line.

Only when they were forced to slow their pace to move along the path through the wood, did he say:

"Is Aline very frightened?"

"She has been amazingly brave," Marisa replied. "She believes that you expect her to show courage and I told her that she represents you."

"Thank you," the Duke said unexpectedly.

They did not speak again until later they came to another wood, and there ahead of them was the mine and to the right of it the miners' houses.

Instinctively they both drew in their horses.

"It is a long time since I have been here," the Duke said. "I have kept the mine open entirely out of sentiment. Perhaps I should have closed it."

"Most of the men are too old to learn any other trade," Marisa said, "but you could close it down slowly over the years, and employ the younger men on other parts of the Estate. You have Stone Masons, you have carpenters and ironmongers, it is easy when they are young to teach them other ways of earning a living. For the smaller children there should be a school."

The Duke did not answer and Marisa went on:

"Perhaps there is one, but I should be surprised if there is."

"Meaning it is something I should have seen to before now" the Duke said.

"Who else?" Marisa asked, "these people are your responsibility."

"As I have said before" the Duke said coldly, "you are very frank, Miss Mitton."

He flicked his horse as he spoke with his whip and moved forward towards the mine. Marisa followed him.

The men were waiting as she had expected them to be, and now there were more of them than there had been before. She knew that the scavengers had returned and she wondered if they had been successful.

She had a feeling that all the fields adjacent to the mine must have been depleted of anything edible long before now.

As they drew nearer to the miners, Marisa saw an almost child-like expression of surprise on their faces. She knew then they had not really believed her when she said she would return with the Duke and alone.

They must, she thought, have expected force, and perhaps after she had left the younger men had reviled the older ones for letting her escape.

Now there was something almost obsequious in the way the men hurried forward eagerly to take the bridle of the Duke's horse and to assist her from the saddle.

She dismounted and the Duke walked up to the elderly man who Marisa had known on her first visit to be the leader and held out his hand.

"I think you must be Cobbler," he said. "I remember your father when I was a little boy and your grandfather served in the mine before him."

"That's right, Your Grace."

"I understand" the Duke went on, "that there is some trouble here. Now suppose you tell me all about it, starting with you, Cobbler and then I will hear what the rest have to say."

The men crowded round him. Marisa turned to the man who was holding her horse.

"I am going to Lady Aline," she said. "Will you help me back into the saddle?"

He did as she asked and she rode the short distance to the houses. There was a boy of about fifteen standing outside one of them. Marisa beckoned to him and he came at once to her horse's head.

She dismounted and as she did so the door opened and Aline came running out.

"You've come back ... you've come back" she cried, "I am so glad! Where is Papa?"

"He is over there," Marisa replied, "and he will be coming to talk to you in a few minutes."

With her arms round Aline she looked over the child's head to Mrs. Crake who had come to the door.

"Thank you for looking after her," she said softly.

"T'were a pleasure, M'am," the woman answered. "Her be a proper little lady."

As Mrs. Crake spoke Marisa heard the rumble of wheels and along the rough track which lay between the houses came the open brake drawn by two horses.

There was a groom in front beside the coachman and another groom behind. Marisa walked towards them and the horses were drawn to a standstill.

As if by magic the doors of every house in the vicinity

opened almost simultaneously and the women and children came hurrying out from inside.

The groom at the back of the brake pulled back the cover and Marisa saw the food beneath it.

There was a cry from one of the women and then as they surged forward the chatter of excited voices grew louder and louder.

Marisa walked to the back of the brake.

"Ask them to listen to me," she said to the groom who was standing up in it.

"Silence!" the man shouted. "Th' lady wishes to speak to you."

He had a loud voice and after he had spoken there was silence except for the whimpering and cries of the children.

"I have brought you food," Marisa said. "Now first I want all the women with small children to receive an egg for each of them, a loaf of bread and a pat of butter. You will tell the grooms how many children you have and then I suggest you go back into your cottages and cook the eggs while we cut up the rest of the food. There will, I am sure, be enough for everyone and there will be milk coming later for the smaller children."

There was a cry of delight from the women which was almost like a cheer.

"I want five of the older women to bring me out their kitchen tables and help cut up the hams" Marisa went on. "For the others there are rabbits and hares to be skinned and cooked. There is also venison which we will cut up and distribute so that every house should have enough to make a stew."

She glanced in the brake as she spoke and added:

"I do not know quite what else there is, but you must help me see that it is divided fairly. Tomorrow I am sure things will be different and there will be money to buy what you need. But for the moment all we can do is see that everyone has something to eat."

This time the women did cheer and although their voices were weak, the sound brought the tears to Marisa's eyes.

Then somehow Marisa and the grooms created order out of what might have been chaos.

The men distributed the eggs, the loaves of bread and portioned the butter. The older women began to slice the hams and cut up the venison.

Marisa was glad that she had thought of bringing knives because the ones from the Castle were sharp and they were able to make the food go further than if it had been hacked away roughly from the bone.

There were unexpected things which Miss Whitcham had included like large pork pies, a huge brawn, a whole cheese and a number of freshly roasted chickens.

Marisa had these cut up and distributed to the mothers of the smallest children. Their gratitude was pathetic.

She had seen, as they walked back to their cottages with the eggs, that the children of five and six years of age had snatched the loaves of bread from their hands and devoured it ravenously, so hungry that they would have eaten anything, even raw meat if they had been allowed to do so.

Finally the brake was empty, but Marisa knew that every house had enough for a large meal.

It was not perhaps much for a full grown man who had been without food for weeks, but at least for tonight no-one would be starving.

The women were cutting up the last of the hams when the Duke accompanied by Cobbler and the other men came from the mine. Aline saw him first.

"Papa!" she cried, "Papa!"

Running from Marisa's side she hurried across the rough ground towards the Duke.

Marisa had been too busy distributing the food to pay any attention to Aline's appearance, but now she wondered what the Duke would think of the child's dirt-stained face and black hands.

Then she decided it would do him good.

At the Castle he viewed life, she thought, from behind a glass window, seeing poverty and privation but not being in touch with it, not realising what it meant in terms of human suffering.

And Aline, like the other children and women of the aristocracy, never rubbed shoulders with the hoi polloi nor had they any idea of the degrading conditions in which the vast majority of the people lived.

Yet, Marisa thought, she had learnt that luxury did not make for happiness, nor a full stomach for contentment.

Perhaps those who were well-bred being more sensitive suffered more than those who were born hardened to it and with a poverty of intellect.

It was a question she could not answer.

She only knew that it was an indescribable anguish to watch the physical or mental purgatory of others. And she longed to alleviate pain wherever she found it.

"Can you not help the Duke?" her heart asked.

"No, not him—not any more!" she cried bitterly, remembering the disgust and condemnation in his voice, as he told her to get out of his sight.

She watched Aline running towards her father and then to her surprise the Duke held out his arms and as Aline ran to him, he picked her up and kissed her.

It was a spontaneous gesture and Marisa knew it was the first time he had ever kissed the child.

Aline put her arms round his neck and the Duke carrying her came towards Marisa.

"I see you have been busy," he said as he reached her side.

"We have divided the food as fairly as we could," Marisa answered not meeting his eyes, "at least the children are fed."

She glanced towards the miners who had followed the Duke and said to Mrs. Cobbler:

"The milk should be here very shortly. It is of course for the younger children. I have asked that more eggs should also be sent with it, and I think there should be more butter, but I doubt if there is any bread left on which to spread it."

"We will manage" Mr. Cobbler said, "His Grace has been most generous."

It seemed to Marisa as if the Duke looked at her with a quizzical smile on his lips, as if he challenged her to find fault.

"I am glad" Marisa said quietly.

"Now I think I must take my daughter home" the Duke said, "it has been rather a long day for her."

He put Aline down as he spoke and held out his hand.

"Goodbye, Cobbler and another time if things go wrong

come yourself and see me at the Castle. I think it would be far better if we talked things over between us."

"I'll do that, Yer Grace," Mr. Cobbler said, "and thank ye for what ye've promised."

"The money should be here first thing in the morning," the Duke said, "and the other matters we discussed will be put in hand immediately."

"Thank ye kindly" Mr. Cobbler answered and the other men behind him murmured their approval.

The Duke's horse and Marisa's were led to their side.

"Shall I take Aline home in the brake?" Marisa asked.

"I think she would rather come with me" the Duke replied.

He spoke to one of the grooms and when he had mounted Samson, the man handed Aline up to him and she sat astride the saddle in front of her father.

"This is exciting, Papa," Marisa heard her say, "I've never ridden such a big horse before."

The other groom helped Marisa into the saddle, then the Duke looked down at the men watching them.

"Goodbye," he said, "I am glad to have met you all."

The men were cheering as they moved away and once again Marisa felt the tears pricking her eyes.

'I must be very tired,' she thought and knew that was the truth.

She had not slept the night before and she had eaten nothing since a light supper before she had gone downstairs to the Library, carrying her manuscript in her hand.

She had almost forgotten the horror of the previous night because she had been so busy all day trying to save Aline and help the miners' children.

Now the humiliation of the Duke's anger and the insulting manner in which he had kissed her encompassed her like a dark fog.

For a few hours she had been in command in a critical situation. She had made decisions, forced people to obey them and accomplished what seemed in retrospect a miracle.

But the moment of glory was over.

She was now just a woman caught out in a disgraceful act. A muckraker, a creature of decadent tastes, whom any decent man would scorn.

She felt again the shock of that moment when she had looked down from the balcony and seen the Duke holding the manuscript in his hand.

It seemed to Marisa a long way back to the Castle. They did not move fast for which she was grateful. Aline was talking excitedly to the Duke, so it was not easy for him to speak to Marisa.

Only as they proceeded through the woods did he say with a slight note of sarcasm in his voice:

"I hope, Miss Mitton, you are satisfied."

"What have you promised them?" Marisa enquired.

"Increased wages and the pay they should have earned during the strike," the Duke answered. "New props for the mine, any safety devices they think essential, and a cottage and a pension for life for the widow and children of the man who died."

Marisa drew a deep breath.

"That is wonderful!"

"I have also suggested that the Estate carpenters should carry out essential repairs in the houses" the Duke continued. "If you and Aline intend visiting such places, I feel there ought to be improvements."

"Not for our sakes, for theirs," Marisa said.

"My intentions are good," the Duke replied, "even though I am quite certain, Miss Mitton, you will find points to criticise."

"I have no wish to do that, Your Grace," Marisa said in a low voice. "I was sure you did not know what was happening."

"But, as you have so clearly pointed out, I was at fault even in being ignorant," the Duke insisted.

"They were very poor, Papa," Aline interposed. "They slept on the floor and had only hard chairs, and even they were broken."

The Duke did not answer and after a moment Aline said:

"I promised the little girls my toys, but I do not think they understood exactly what toys are. They did not have any in their houses, not a single one."

"We shall have to alter that in the future," the Duke said.

"Miss Mitton said I could take them all my old dolls,"

Aline went on, "but I would like to buy them some new ones too. Can I do that, Papa?"

"You shall do whatever you like," the Duke said.

Marisa had the idea there was a touch of embarrassment in his voice.

They were now through the wood and he set Samson at a brisk trot towards the Castle. They still had some way to go and when they reached the gravel swept in front of the steps, Aline was silent and Marisa knew she must be very tired.

She had missed her rest, she had been given no lunch and she had been very frightened. By the time the Duke drew up his horse beside the steps of the Castle, Aline was almost asleep.

A footman lifted her down from the saddle.

"Carry her straight upstairs," the Duke ordered.

Another footman helped Marisa to alight. As she reached the ground she suddenly felt curiously unsteady.

Her tiredness had been increasing during the last part of the ride home, and now she wondered whether she would have the strength to walk up the steps.

The Duke had already moved up ahead of her, and as she reached the Hall it seemed to her it was filled with people.

She could hear Miss Whitcham's high excited voice and she felt as if it was far, far away and she could not breathe.

Instinctively, hardly knowing what she was doing, Marisa pulled her hat from her head.

Then the Hall seemed to be whirling round her and the darkness came up from the floor and covered her.

She was at the end of a long tunnel, there was a faint light, she was still moving.

She thought she must be riding and then she realised she was held in someone's arms. She thought she must have fainted and like a flash of lightning she knew who carried her.

She had a feeling of security, of safety and comfort that she had never known before. The Duke held her closely and yet so easily that she was aware it was no effort.

He moved steadily and without opening her eyes she

knew they were climbing up the second flight of stairs which led to the School-Room floor.

Last night the Duke had kissed her and she had been afraid, now it was almost like finding Heaven to be so near to him and to know the strength of his arms.

She wanted to hide her face against his shoulder.

Instead she lay still, thinking to herself that she would never know this moment again, never again feel the beat of his heart against her cheek.

Someone opened the bed-room door and Marisa, still with her eyes closed, felt him carry her across the room.

He set her down very gently against the pillows and she resisted an absurd impulse to put out her arms and hold on to him.

"Put her to bed," she heard the Duke say in his deep voice, "she is completely exhausted. And try to persuade her to have something to eat."

"Yes, Your Grace."

Marisa knew it was the Housekeeper who spoke. She thought the Duke must have turned away and her eyelids fluttered for a moment.

Then she felt his hand on hers and he said quietly:

"I am deeply grateful, Miss Mitton."

'He must have known I was conscious', she thought in a sudden panic, and heard his footsteps cross the room and go down the stairs.

She was so tired that she let herself be undressed.

One of the maids slipped a nightgown over her head and took the pins from her hair. They brought her food and to please them she drank a little soup and ate a mouthful of chicken.

She was almost too tired to swallow and it was with a sense of relief that finally she found herself left alone and immediately fell into a deep dreamless slumber.

She must have slept for many hours for when finally she woke the room was dark.

She lay thinking over what had occurred, remembering more vividly than anything else the feel of the Duke's arms as he carried her up the stairs.

She had thought when she had tried to leave the Castle the previous day that her last memory would be of him cursing her and the anger in his voice when he had told her to get out of his sight.

But now she knew that she would never be able to forget the comfort and security of his hold, of knowing that he had carried her upstairs as if she was only a child and the gentleness of him as he lay her down on the bed.

"I am deeply grateful, Miss Mitton," he had said.

There had been a kindness and a gratitude in his voice which made her want to cry.

Then as her love for him surged over her like a great wave of the sea, she remembered how he denounced her for writing her book.

She recalled the contempt and disgust in his voice, and she knew that he had been kind to her now only because of the manner in which she had handled the miners.

But there was nothing changed between them: he loathed and despised her, and nothing could alter that, nothing she could do or say.

She knew then that she could not bear to see him again.

She must leave the Castle as she had intended to do the day before, and she thought if she did not do so there was no doubt that he would dismiss her.

That she could not bear!

Instinctively, at the thought of the condemnation on his face and the harshness in his voice, Marisa sat up in bed and reached for the matches.

She lit a candle and saw by the clock on the mantelpiece that it was nearly five o'clock. Soon it would be light, and before the whole Castle was awake she must be gone.

Marisa rose and dressed herself.

She felt rather shaky on her legs and a little light in her head, but otherwise the night's rest had swept away the worse of her fatigue.

She put on her blue travelling clothes. One of her trunks had been brought upstairs last night obviously so that the housemaids could find her a nightgown to wear.

Marisa considered for a moment and then decided that all the gowns she had been given by Kitty Berrington to wear at the Castle were no longer important.

They had been given her for a special purpose and that was over. She would leave everything behind.

Perhaps later she would write to Miss Whitcham and ask her to send her baggage to her Aunt's house in London. Until then she decided that her trunks contained nothing that was really necessary to her.

She put her brush and comb into the leather bag which contained her jewellery, remembering that before she arrived it had held the manuscript of her book.

Ready dressed Marisa took from the drawer in which she had put it yesterday the letter she had written to Aline.

Holding the candle in her hand, she walked across the landing and laid the letter on the School-Room table. Then she went downstairs and out through a side-door which led towards the stables.

She could hear the housemaids moving in the Great Hall and there was a chatter of voices from the kitchen-quarters, but she met no-one.

On reaching the stables she found two of the younger grooms sweeping out the horse-boxes.

They looked up in surprise when she appeared.

"I want a carriage immediately to take me to the Halt" she said. "I have to go to London."

"Very good, Miss."

If the grooms thought it strange that someone living in the Castle should come to the stables rather than send a message, they did not show it.

In a very short space of time the grooms had dragged the Brougham out into the yard and the horses were between the shafts.

A coachman hastily donning his uniform climbed on the box and picked up the reins, and Marisa was handed into the carriage.

She sank back against the cushions as the horses drew out of the yard.

This time she did not look back at the Castle or at the beauty of the surroundings. She had, instead, the feeling that she was escaping.

Not just going away, but escaping from something tenacious, something that was holding on to her, something which seemed to be pleading with her not to go.

It was an absurd feeling, something which she could

not even explain to herself, and yet it was there. She felt she must urge the horses to go faster.

She almost expected to hear the sound of hooves coming up from behind to command the Coachman to bring the carriage to a standstill, to tell her she must return.

It was as if she moved in a dream, a dream of her own imaginings, a dream that was so vivid that she knew her heart was beating tumultuously and her breath came quickly as if she had been running for a long way.

They reached the Halt and the groom opened the door.

"What time is there a train due?" Marisa asked.

"I don't think th' milk train has been through yet, Miss," the groom replied.

He went ahead of her as he spoke and put up the signal. It was crimson against the pale morning sky.

"Hurry, hurry, hurry" Marisa wanted to cry aloud.

It was cold waiting on the little platform and she felt herself shiver.

The November wind seemed to find its way under her travelling-cloak and she could feel the frosty air cold against her cheeks.

There was an astringent quality about it which seemed to strengthen her determination to get away, to be free, to leave behind the past that was curling itself like tendrils round her.

She had resisted a temptation to look back along the road by which they had come. Who would be following her, who could possibly wish to prevent her leaving?

Then she heard the whistle of the train in the distance and saw a puff of black smoke beyond a distant bend.

"That'll be th' milk train a coming, Miss," the groom announced. "There be usually two carriages attached to it and not many passengers at this hour of th' day."

He watched the train for a moment before he said:

"You'll be a coming back this evening, Miss. Have you any idea what time you'd like us to meet you?"

For a moment Marisa was surprised at the question, and then she realised that as she had no luggage, he thought she was going to London just for the day.

She did not know why, but it was hard to answer him truthfully and yet she managed to do so.

"I shall not be coming back," she said quite firmly.

Chapter Nine

Marisa walked across the floor of her father's Study and stood for a moment at the window looking out onto the unkempt garden.

It was a dull November day. There had been a sharp frost during the night which had brought the last remaining leaves from the trees, so that the branches were already gaunt against the sky.

The sombre greyness of the scene seemed to be echoed in her heart. With a little shiver Marisa turned from the window to walk to the fire, holding out her hands to the flames flickering above the dry logs and wondering why she felt that nothing would ever warm the cold within herself.

"I have a frozen heart" she had told her aunt.

She was wearing one of the two black dresses she had bought in a shop in St. Albans when her father died.

It was of cheap material but it could not disguise the soft curves of her body and it threw into prominence the dazzling whiteness of her skin and the vivid red of her hair.

When she had risen this morning she had twisted her hair into a knot at the back of her head and pinned it hastily turning away from her own reflection in the mirror.

She knew only too well she would see eyes stricken and miserable, dark lines beneath them from a sleepless night and a mouth which was still trembling with the memory of the bitter tears she had shed into her pillow.

She had come home like a wounded animal, seeking the sanctuary of what was familiar and yet finding little to comfort her in the memories of the past.

It was impossible not to be haunted by her father's voice proclaiming against Society, ranting on and on against those who bore a noble name, seizing on every particle of scandal and using it to illustrate his conviction that every ill from which the country suffered was directly the fault of the aristocracy.

"How could I have been so foolish as to believe him?" Marisa asked herself now.

Yet she knew he had indoctrinated her with his own animosity so thoroughly that she would have been a phenomenon had she been strong enough to remain uninfluenced by his obsession.

And yet overnight it seemed that all the hatred she had harboured within herself, all the convictions in which she had believed so earnestly, all her desires for revenge, had vanished as if at the touch of a magic wand.

She had no need to ask herself what had caused the transformation, she knew only too well—it was love.

As she travelled away from the Castle towards London, she had hoped that having escaped she could cut the weeks she had spent at Vox out of her life and in time forget they had ever happened.

But the further she was carried away from the Duke, the more agonising she found it to be apart from him.

How could she ever forget that he had twice held her in his arms, once in anger and once in compassion.

She had only to shut her eyes to feel herself being carried up the stairs, to recall the closeness of him, to hear the gentleness and sincerity in his voice when he thanked her.

Only to think of it made the weak tears start to her eyes.

It was with a super-human effort that she prevented herself from breaking down and sobbing until at last she was home and alone in her own familiar little bed at Berrington Park.

The servants, old Bates and his wife, had not been surprised to see her:

"We were a wondering when we'd hear from you, M'Lady," Bates had said.

They cooked her an evening meal, but Marisa had been unable to eat it, and had hurried from the dining-table into her own bed-room to lock herself in and cry until she was utterly and completely exhausted.

When she had risen this morning she had told herself that she had to be brave.

Life must go on, and even those who suffered from a broken heart would find something to occupy their mind as the years passed by.

Yet she wondered how she could live with only her memories.

It was not only that she missed the Duke—and the agony of her love was such that she could not even think of him without the fear of renewed weeping—but she also missed Aline.

She had grown to love the child and it had been a joy that she had never known before in her lonely companion-less life to change the child's outlook, to lead her, to guide her, to teach her and to see so quickly the results of her labours.

Aline was the Duke's daughter: she had his obstinacy and his determination, but she had also much of his charm and his generosity of thought.

She had as well the quality which the Duke had shown in dealing with the miners, his ability to understand other people's difficulties and other people's problems.

Aline had all these things in a smaller degree, and if she was properly influenced from her childhood she would, Marisa was certain, grow up into a woman of character.

But would she be taught in the right way?

It was a separate torture of its own to wonder if a new governess would undo all the good she had done for Aline.

Then Marisa remembered that at least she had been able to bring to the little girl the affection of her father.

There was no doubt that the Duke's whole attitude towards his daughter had changed, once he had realised that she was in fact his own child, and that the lie he had believed for so many years was a fantasy or the revenge of a sick woman.

Father and daughter would grow closer to each other, Marisa thought, as time went by.

But it was a stab of pain to realise that she would not

be there to see them or even know that they were through
her efforts united in a special relationship.

Holding out her hands to the flames Marisa forced herself to think of her own immediate problems.

She heard the door open behind her and old Bates, who
was long past retiring age, came shuffling into the room.

"I came to ask what you'd like for luncheon, M'Lady?"
he said in a quavering voice.

"I do not want anything," Marisa answered.

"Now, M'Lady, there's no use in talking like that,"
Bates said with the scolding familiarity of an ancient
family retainer. "It's worried Mrs. Bates and I are about
your Ladyship, and that's the truth. You ate nothing last
night and you left your breakfast untouched this morning.
Mrs. Bates took real trouble to pick you out a brown
egg!"

"I know, Bates," Marisa replied, "and please thank her
for me, but I am not hungry."

"We wonders if you are a sickening for someout," Bates
suggested.

"No," Marisa answered, "I am all right, just tired."

"You're looking, M'Lady, as if a puff of wind would
blow you away, and that's a fact."

The old man paused, and as Marisa said nothing he
went on:

"Mrs. Bates was thinking of making a Shepherds Pie
for luncheon. It was something His Late Lordship was
very partial to, as you well knows."

"That will be very nice" Marisa said, "and I will try to
eat some of it."

"I'll tell Mrs. Bates, it will please her, M'Lady, it will
really."

The old man had made as if to leave the room when
Marisa asked:

"What plans are being made about the house, Bates? I
have not heard what my uncle has decided."

"I understands His Lordship is going to have a lot of
decorations done" Bates replied, "and there's some talk,
M'Lady, of the workmen coming in the week after next,
but I haven't heard details as yet. 'Tis only what I have
learnt from the letter His Lordship wrote to the new Farm
Manager."

"There is a new Farm Manager?" Marisa questioned.

"Yes, M'Lady. He moved in to Coomb's Farm a week ago. A nice-spoken man and I hopes he'll make some improvements. There is plenty of room for 'em."

"There is indeed," Marisa agreed. "And what is going to happen to you and Mrs. Bates?"

"His Lordship is offering us a cottage in the village, M'Lady. We're looking forward to our retirement, Mrs. Bates and I. Forty-nine years we've been in service and we're getting too old to carry on and that's the truth."

"I shall miss you, Bates," Marisa said. "The Park will not seem the same without you here."

"Will you be living here, M'Lady?" Bates enquired.

Marisa shook her head.

"No indeed. I plan this afternoon to visit Miss Meadfield. I am hoping that I can stay with her for a while until I find something to do."

"And I'm sure, M'Lady, she'll be real pleased to see you," Bates said. "She called a few days after you had left for London."

"Oh did she?" Marisa exclaimed. "I am sorry to have missed her."

"She was sorry to miss you, M'Lady. To tell the truth Miss Meadfield finds it over lonely a living on her own."

"But she was so anxious to retire!" Marisa exclaimed. "It was not that she was old, she cannot now be more than sixty. But she always said when she left here that she had finished with teaching."

"People talks like that" Bates said with the wisdom of old age. "But what it comes down to, M'Lady, is that when they have nothing to do they find time lying heavy on their hands. It is not as if Miss Meadfield is in ill health. From the way she was speaking I thinks she is considering taking pupils again, if there are any who need instruction in Little Minns."

"Well she will not be lonely if I am with her," Marisa said.

"No, that's a fact" Bates agreed. "Miss Meadfield was so fond of you, M'Lady, that I've always thought, and so has Mrs. Bates, that the reason she gave up teaching was that she could not bear to put another child in your place."

"I cannot quite believe that" Marisa smiled.

"It were a pity, M'Lady, there wasn't some younger members of the family for her to take on when Your Ladyship were too old for lessons."

"That is something I have regretted all my life," Marisa sighed. "I was a very lonely child."

"You were indeed, M'Lady. What with his late Lordship disliking visitors and not wishing to have any company in the house, it weren't a natural life, as one might say, for a young girl."

"Perhaps it was not," Marisa said.

She turned her face towards the fire.

"You can be quite sure, M'Lady, that Miss Meadfield will welcome you with open arms," Bates went on. "Now if Your Ladyship will excuse me I'll just go and tell Mrs. Bates that you fancy a bit of Shepherd's Pie. 'Tis always been one of her best dishes."

The old man shuffled away towards the door and Marisa sat staring into the fire.

She would go to Miss Meadfield, she decided, she would make her home there and she would try to think of something that she could do.

"Anything" she told herself fiercely, "anything except writing!"

That was forbidden, that was something she could never contemplate again.

She thought of her manuscript burning in the fire in her bed-room at Vox, the pages curling over in the heat and gradually becoming black, the noise of the flames as they roared up the chimney.

Then she could remember the charred remains filling the fireplace as she had thrown herself down on the hearth-rug in agony of self-accusation.

"A muck raker and a culminator!" The words were engraved on her heart.

How could she have sunk so low? How could she have let her father influence her to do anything so despicable?

It was contradictory to all her romantic dreams, all the loveliness of the wild world outside the house which had been her secret consolation and delight all through her adolescence?

What had been true to her then were the nymphs which

rose waif-like in the mist over the stream at the bottom of the garden.

She had believed in the elves which lingered in the shadows in the woods and rustled amongst the leaves in the trees and she had dreamt every night of deeds of valour in history and in legend that had thrilled her when she had read about them.

These had been far more real than the shadowy social puppets who must dance at her father's command, but had in fact only been words written in the ink which flowed from her pen.

She heard the door open behind her and Bates's voice say:

"A gentleman to see you, M'Lady."

She thought it must be the new Farm Manager, and afraid there might be tears on her cheeks, she drew her handkerchief quickly from the belt of her dress to wipe them away before she turned her head.

Then slowly, hoping the new arrival would not have noticed her action, she turned round and was suddenly transfixed.

It was the Duke who stood there!

He seemed unnaturally tall and large in the small room. He was dressed conventionally in dark London clothes in which she had not seen him before, and she thought for one moment in a wild panic that she could not speak to him, that she must run away and hide.

But the door was behind him and a pride she had always possessed came to her rescue, so she summoned up courage to put up her chin and face him.

"Why are you here . . .?" she began.

Then a terrifying thought struck her and she ejaculated.

"Aline!"

"Aline is all right," the Duke replied soothingly and saw the fear vanish from her eyes. "She has asked me to bring you back to Vox."

For a moment Marisa stared at him, then she turned away.

"No!"

The word seemed to be louder than she had intended so that she felt as if it echoed round the Study.

"Yesterday morning when we found you had gone" the

Duke continued, "Aline said to me, 'I love you Papa, but it is very empty here without Miss Mitton. Will you bring her back to us?' "

It seemed to Marisa the Duke had come nearer to her as he spoke, and now instinctively afraid of his closeness she walked away from the fireplace towards her desk which stood between the windows.

"It is . . . impossible," she said in a strangled voice.

"Why?" the Duke enquired.

She did not answer and after a moment he asked:

"Why did you run away?"

"You . . . told me . . . to go."

"I spoke while I was in a rage and you knew I did not mean it. I thought you might have forgotten my anger after what happened the next day—when you saved Aline."

Marisa said nothing. She had rested one hand on the desk and was staring down at the blotter as if she had never seen it before.

"Will you not forget all the differences between us and come back to the Castle?" the Duke asked. "We need you desperately—Aline and I."

The kindness in his voice was more difficult to combat than anything Marisa had known before.

Her head was bent and a tear she could not control splashed down on the desk in front of her.

She was trying to find her voice when the Duke asked:

"Why are you crying?"

"I am . . . not" she answered almost fiercely, but as she spoke another tear joined the first one on the desk.

"Look at me, Marisa," the Duke said and she did not notice he had used her Christian name.

"If you are not crying," he went on as she did not move, "I want you to look at me."

"I . . . cannot" she whispered.

"Why? And why will you not come back to Vox? You know how much we need you."

"No . . . no" Marisa cried and there was a frantic tone in her voice.

"Tell me the reason," the Duke pleaded.

He was now standing just behind her and she could feel the closeness of him. She was trembling, and as the tears welled into her eyes with a sudden effort she told the truth.

"I am . . . so . . . ashamed" she stammered.

She felt his hands on her shoulders. He turned her round and she shut her eyes.

The tears were running down her pale cheeks, her mouth was bleared and quivering and then somehow, she did not know how it happened, she was crying against his shoulder and his lips were against her hair.

"Will you try to forgive me for all the cruel, unkind and untrue things I said to you?" he asked in his deep voice. "I did not then understand, Marisa, about your father, about the life you had led here. I was only furious that anyone so beautiful as you should be involved in anything so unpleasant."

"I have . . . burnt . . . it . . . I have . . . burnt the . . . book," Marisa sobbed. "But you were . . . right! I was . . . muck-raking. It was despicable . . . beastly . . . and I am so . . . humiliated."

"Darling, darling, forget it," the Duke pleaded. "You must know that I have loved you since the first moment I saw you!"

Marisa was suddenly very still.

It was as if everything up to this moment had been happening in a dream; but now this was reality, she was hearing him say such words as she had thought never to hear spoken to her.

"It is not . . . true?" she whispered.

"It is the truth."

Very gently he put his fingers under her chin and turned her face up to his.

The tears were standing on the ends of her long eyelashes and her eyes seemed very big in her little face. They looked up at him searchingly, questioningly.

As if he understood, he said softly.

"I love you."

Then his lips were on hers.

He kissed her gently, very gently as if he was afraid to hurt her, and then his mouth grew more passionate more possessive until she quivered in his arms and felt as if he drew her very soul from her body and made it his.

The room seemed to whirl round them, the world disappeared.

There was no unhappiness, no trouble, no horror, only a golden enchanted place where they were alone together—a man and a woman who had come through deep waters and great tribulations to find each other.

"God how I love you" the Duke exclaimed hoarsely.

He drew Marisa to the sofa in front of the fire, still holding her close as if he was afraid she might escape him.

"Is this . . . really . . . true?" she asked after a moment.

"That is what I am asking myself too," he said. "If you only knew how frantic I was when I realised you had gone and I had no idea how to find you!"

"I had to go . . . away" Marisa answered. "I thought you . . . despised me."

"How could you think anything so foolish?" the Duke asked. "I have thought about you, wanted you and loved you ever since I found you and Aline shooting that pheasant out of season. But you looked at me with such dislike in your eyes! I could not understand it."

"I made myself . . . hate you long before I came to Vox," Marisa said, "and then when . . . I saw you . . ."

She paused.

"What happened then?" the Duke asked.

"I tried to go on hating you and . . . failed" she whispered, "I think I must have . . . loved you from the . . . very first but I did not know . . . it was love."

His lips were on hers again and she could not speak for a long time. Then at length with her head against his shoulder she asked:

"How did you . . . find me?"

"My only hope of tracing you was through Lady Berrington, who had written originally to recommend you" he answered. "I managed to see her yesterday evening. She had been away and did not return home until five o'clock, otherwise I should have come to you last night. Of course I had no idea then that she was your aunt."

"And she told you who I was?" Marisa asked in surprise.

"She lied most convincingly at first," the Duke answered with a smile, "you had frightened her considerably with the book you proposed writing."

"I am ... sorry," Marisa murmured and turned her face against his shoulder.

"I think we can reassure Lady Berrington that such fears are now groundless" the Duke said. "But she was so apprehensive, that for a long time she disclaimed any knowledge of you or your whereabouts."

"How did you persuade her?"

"I told her that I wished to find Miss Mitton because I intended to make her my wife."

"You told her what?" Marisa cried.

"You must marry me, my darling, I cannot live without you."

The Duke's arms tightened round her and with his eyes twinkling he continued.

"If you mean to refuse me, may I suggest that you are behaving at this moment in a somewhat reprehensible manner for a governess!"

Marisa gave a little choked laugh that was half a sob. Then she said:

"But you cannot ... want to ... marry me ... not really ... knowing what I feel about ... the social world."

"Of which you know nothing!" the Duke said. "Only the sordid scandals with which your father indoctrinated you. Kitty Berrington told me how fanatical he was on the subject, and I can understand it if your mother was as lovely as you."

"I am not beautiful like Mama." Marisa said.

"I do not believe anyone could be more beautiful" the Duke said, "and I know only too well what your father must have felt when he lost her."

He held Marisa closer still and said:

"I am never going to lose you again, my precious. If you only knew how distraught I was on my way to London, and when at first I believed your aunt was speaking the truth when she said she had no idea where I could find you."

"And what did you ... feel when you ... knew where ... I was?" Marisa asked.

"Do you really want me to tell you that?" he enquired, "because darling, you are well aware you are the woman for whom I have been searching all my life. The woman who was meant for me, the woman who is the other part of myself. We have found each other, and God knows I am more grateful than I can ever put into words."

He looked down into Marisa's face, at her eyes alight with happiness and he was kissing her again.

Kissing her with a passion that made her heart turn over in her breast, kissing her until a flame within her leapt to meet the fire she saw in his eyes.

Then his lips were on her eyes, her cheeks, and finally on her neck.

She felt a little quiver run through her.

"No . . . no" she whispered, "no . . ."

"No?" he questioned, "do you dislike my doing that?"

"Not . . . dislike" Marisa answered, "but it makes me feel . . . so excited . . . so wild."

She hesitated, then asked:

"Is that . . . wrong?"

"Wrong" the Duke repeated. "How old are you, my darling?"

"I am twenty, nearly twenty-one" Marisa answered.

"Oh my little love" the Duke exclaimed, "I believed you were twenty-four, as Miss Whitcham told me you were. I have been so crazily jealous of all the men who must have loved you in the past and perhaps kissed you."

"No-one has ever . . . kissed me but . . . you."

"You are still only a child, innocent and unawakened" the Duke said, "and I have so much to teach you, so much my precious that I want you to learn about love."

"You said when we . . . first met there might be . . . things we could . . . teach each other."

"I thought when we talked together in the Study that you were the most beautiful creature I had ever seen in my life. There was something about you which drew me to you, which made me feel that I must hold on to you that I must never lose you, that you must be mine. But I was afraid of the condemnation I saw in your eyes, the coldness I heard in your voice."

"I was . . . attracted by you too," Marisa murmured, "but I told myself that I . . . hated all that . . . you stood for."

"And now—what do you feel about me now?" the Duke asked.

She smiled up at him and he thought he had never seen anyone look so radiantly happy.

"I love . . . you. I love you with . . . all my heart."

He swept her into his arms but even as she thrilled at the touch of his lips, he raised his head.

"When I told your Aunt I wished to marry you" he said, "she instantly began to plan a full-scale Society wedding."

"Oh no!" Marisa exclaimed, "no! I could not bear it."

". . . in a year's time when you come out of mourning," the Duke continued.

He looked into Marisa's eyes and there was a question in them.

"Must we . . . wait so . . . long?" she whispered.

"Do you really think I could wait as long as that for you?" the Duke enquired. "Do you think I will risk losing you again? I want you now, at once. Because I adore you, my dearest heart, and I want you beside me, to know you are mine, my own and my wife."

"But what can we do?"

To Marisa's surprise the Duke rose from the sofa and pulled her to her feet.

"Go and put on your travelling-clothes," he said. "I know you have nothing to pack because your trunks are all still at Vox."

"Where are we going?" Marisa asked.

"To London," he said, "to be married."

"Now . . . today?"

"I will get a Special Licence" he said, "and we can be married in London at a Registry Office or in the private Chapel at Vox."

"Oh, please, at Vox!" Marisa cried. "Besides we must tell Aline first. I would not want her to be jealous of me, as she has been of all the other women you have loved."

"I have never loved anyone but you," the Duke replied. "You are not to speak of them in the same breath as yourself, do you hear?"

He lifted Marisa's face up to his as he spoke, then looking down into her eyes he said:

"We both have things to forget. Let us forget them,

bury them in the past! There are so many things we can do in the future, you and I together."

"Together," Marisa whispered.

Then she slipped from his arms and hurried upstairs to her bed-room.

It did not take her long to put on the smart blue travelling-dress and cloak in which she had come home.

She threw the black dress she had been wearing down on the chair and thought it was symbolic of all that was dark and unhappy in the past and which she was discarding for ever.

She felt as if there were wings on her feet and in a moment she was downstairs again.

The Duke was waiting for her in the Study and as she entered the room he held out his arms and she ran towards him, her face alight with happiness.

"I love you, I love you," he said.

Then his lips were on hers and she knew they were already one person and nothing could divide them.

They did not arrive at the Castle until late in the evening.

The Duke had sent a telegram to say on what train they would be travelling and a carriage was waiting at the Halt with the usual number of footmen to see to their comfort.

Once they were inside the carriage Marisa slipped her hand into the Duke's.

"Happy my darling?" he asked.

"Very happy!"

"And not too tired? You seemed to find so much to do in London."

"I wanted to buy myself a wedding-gown, something that really belonged to me, and also a dress for Aline to wear at our wedding and several other dresses far more suitable for her years."

"I can see that if you think so much about my daughter I could easily become jealous of her," the Duke said teasingly.

"I am worried that she might dislike the thought of my marrying you," Marisa said. "But I know she will be happy with Miss Meadfield. And you could see as soon as we asked her to come and teach Aline, how glad she was to come out of retirement."

"I think really she was happy at the thought of being near you," the Duke said.

"She promised to arrive tomorrow morning," Marisa went on. "I would like to introduce her to Aline before we leave for our honeymoon."

"We will do exactly what pleases you my sweet" the Duke replied. "As long as I can take you with me to France and on to Italy where we can be alone together, that is all I ask of the future."

"Everyone will be very angry they have been done out of an important Society wedding" Marisa said.

"Do we care what everyone says or thinks?" the Duke asked scornfully. "All that matters, Marisa, is that there should be as little gossip as possible. We will be away at least three or four months, and I shall announce that our marriage has taken place just before we return."

"You think we can trust Aunt Kitty to keep such a momentous secret until then?" Marisa asked with a smile.

"I think she is so delighted that you are becoming respectable by marrying me, that she will agree to any condition we impose upon her!"

"You are very puffed up with your own consequence" Marisa teased.

The Duke laughed and kissed her.

But Marisa was serious as they drove down the drive and saw the Castle ahead of them. The lights in the windows were glowing golden in the twilight, and the great edifice was warm and welcoming.

Marisa knew as she looked at it that her future home already occupied a very important place of her heart.

They alighted at the front door and Aline came running down the steps.

"Papa has brought you back!" she cried and flung her arms round Marisa.

"Yes darling, he has brought me home," Marisa answered.

"I am glad, so very very glad!" Aline said. "I was so afraid he would not find you. You are clever, Papa!"

She turned towards her father as she spoke, looking at him a little shyly. The Duke bent down to kiss her.

There was a smile on Turner's grave face as they entered the Hall and Aline holding the Duke by one hand and Marisa by the other drew them into the Drawing-room.

"Turner has put drinks for you in here, Papa, and there is tea for Miss Mitton because I know she likes it best."

"How sweet of you to think of it," Marisa smiled.

But her eyes were a little apprehensive as the Duke shut the door and came across to the sofa where she and Aline were sitting.

There was a silence, and as if Aline sensed that something unusual was about to happen, she looked up enquiringly at Marisa.

"Your Papa has something to tell you, darling."

"What is it?" Aline asked.

"You told me to find Miss Mitton and bring her back to you" the Duke began.

"And you found her" Aline interrupted excitedly. "I am so glad and happy, Papa."

"I found her," the Duke continued, "but I am rather worried, Aline. As you know, she has run away from us once, she might do so again."

There was an expression of dismay on the child's face as she turned towards Marisa.

"You won't leave us now you have come back Miss Mitton? You must promise faithfully to stay."

"I have thought of a better idea," the Duke went on, "than asking for promises."

"What is it?" Aline enquired.

"You see," the Duke said choosing his words carefully, "governesses can give notice, they can leave when they want to, and one cannot hold them. So I thought the only way we can be quite certain of keeping Miss Mitton with us is if I ask her to marry me."

"To marry you?" Aline exclaimed. "You mean she would be your wife?"

"She would be my wife," the Duke repeated quietly.

Aline looked from one to the other.

"Then if you are my Papa, Miss Mitton would be my Mama, wouldn't she?"

"Yes, Aline. That is what she would be," the Duke said.

"I would like that! I would like that very much indeed!" Aline cried and flung her arms round Marisa's neck hugging her.

Marisa held the little girl close to her and raised her eyes full of tears towards the Duke. He smiled down at her and in that moment it seemed to Marisa that she had come into a kingdom of her own.

She gave a sigh of relief and happiness.

"And now, Aline," she said, "we have a surprise for you. Your Papa and I are to be married this evening and we want you to be the only person there."

"Married here in the Castle!" Aline exclaimed.

"In the Chapel," Marisa said, "and I have bought you a special dress to wear and several other dresses too, which will make you look older than the ones you are wearing at the moment."

Aline threw her arms round her neck again.

"Oh, I love you! I love you so much!"

"We have not much time," the Duke said, "so, Aline, will you go and tell Turner that the gardeners are to decorate the Chapel with flowers from the greenhouses."

"Yes of course I will tell him" Aline said, "and I will tell Chef that you must have a wedding cake."

"I doubt if there will be time" Marisa smiled, "but perhaps he can concoct something delectable."

"I will tell him! I will tell everybody."

Aline suddenly put her arms round her father's waist and hugged him.

"It is all so exciting, Papa, and I am terribly glad you are going to marry darling Miss Mitton."

Then she had run excitedly from the room leaving Marisa and the Duke alone. He held out his hands to her.

"You see, my precious" he said, "you worried quite unnecessarily."

"I love your daughter," Marisa answered.

"And you have taught me to love her," he said. "That is one of the lessons I have already had from you."

"I must go and get ready. How soon before we will be married?"

The Duke drew his gold watch from the pocket of his waistcoat.

"I sent the Vicar, who is also my private Chaplain, a

telegram from London telling him to meet me here at
7.30" he replied. "That gives you over an hour to make
yourself look beautiful."

"I will try," Marisa said.

"It will not be a very difficult task," the Duke answered
his eyes on her face, "ask Miss Whitcham for the family
lace veil and the flowered tiara which all the Duchesses
wear on special occasions."

Marisa looked up at him.

"You are sure ... quite sure ... that you are doing the
... right thing?"

"In marrying you?" the Duke questioned. "I know it is
the only right thing I have ever done in my whole life.
And, darling, there are so many things that we are going
to do in the future that are both right and good, not only
for ourselves, but for those for whom we have a responsibility."

She knew he was thinking of the miners. She moved
closer to him and felt his arms hold her against his heart.

"But before we can think of anyone else" he said, "I
think it is only fair that we should think of ourselves.
That is why I want to take you away alone, Marisa. There
is so much I want to learn about you, so much I want to
know."

"And there is so much I want to know about you too,"
Marisa answered. "I had no idea, until Mr. Arthur Balfour told me, how clever you are."

"I see it will not only be a honeymoon, but a voyage of
discovery," the Duke smiled.

He kissed her gently, and Marisa left him and went upstairs. As she reached the top of the staircase she heard
him giving orders in the Hall in a voice she knew was
deep with happiness.

On the landing she found Miss Whitcham.

"Oh, Miss Mitton!" she exclaimed, "Aline has told us
the good news: I can hardly believe it, it is most exciting,
quite marvellous and I do hope you and His Grace will be
very happy."

"We will be" Marisa smiled.

"You will be sleeping in here now," Miss Whitcham
told her.

She led the way across the landing and opened the door of the big State Bed-room.

Marisa had learnt when she was exploring the Castle, that it was always used by the brides of the Dukes of Milverley, and it contained the famous carved gilt furniture made for the Castle in the Reign of Charles II.

Resplendant with fat cupids entwined with lover's knots, there were also cupids on the painted ceiling and on the gold sconces holding the candles which lit the room.

Marisa looked round and said softly.

"I feel that many brides have been happy here."

"As I know you will be happy," Miss Whitcham added.

She hesitated a moment and then said hesitatingly.

"Of course you may not wish me to remain on when you return from your honeymoon. It has been different while the Duke had no wife to run the Castle."

Marisa looked down at the anxiety in the elderly woman's eyes and with a new understanding she recognised the anxiety and fear that lay behind the words.

She knew too, that if her new found love had not taught her, she would not have recognised as she did now, that Miss Whitcham's garrulousness and desire for gossip stemmed only from her loneliness and the frustration of being an old maid.

Realising Miss Whitcham's whole future hung on her answer, she said gently, as the Duke's mother had said before her.

"What would we do without you, Whitchy?"

Then she turned away so she would not see the tears spring into the Secretary's eyes.

The Housekeeper and the housemaids came bustling into the room with their congratulations. Miss Whitcham produced the family veil that was so fine that it might have been made by fairy fingers.

The flowered tiara was the most beautiful piece of jewellery that Marisa had ever seen.

The new white gown that she had bought in London was unpacked and laid on the bed and Aline, dancing about in an almost hysterical state of excitement, took her new dress upstairs to change into it.

"I would like a bath please," Marisa said to the Housekeeper.

The fire burning beneath the marble mantelshelf and the lighted candles cast a golden glow over the carved gold furniture.

There were soft shadows inside the embroidered curtains of the huge four-poster which had ostrich feather fronds reaching towards the ceiling. Behind the lace-edged pillows, gold Cupids supported a heart.

"I must leave you to change," Miss Whitcham said in an embarrassed voice.

Then she added:

"His Grace has given orders that only Aline can attend the ceremony, but I think you will understand that everyone in the Castle will be deeply hurt if they cannot be present. You see, many of them who have worked here all their lives, feel they are almost part of the family."

Marisa did not speak and Miss Whitcham said hastily.

"Perhaps I ought not to have spoken! You must forgive me, Miss Mitton."

"Wait a moment," Marisa said, "wait here until I come back."

She went from the room and ran down the stairs. There was no sign of the Duke in the Hall but she found him in the Study speaking to Turner.

The Butler withdrew as she appeared and Marisa ran across the room to the Duke's side.

"What has happened?" he asked quickly.

"There is nothing wrong" Marisa replied, "it is only that I have just realised that everyone in the household wishes to be present at our wedding."

The Duke did not speak and she went on:

"You see, darling, I do understand because they have been here for so long that they feel they are part of the family—your family, which they have served for generations."

The Duke smiled.

"Our family," he corrected, "yours and mine, my darling."

He kissed her and said with a note of gaiety in his voice which Marisa had never heard before:

"Let them all come! After all, as you say, it is very much a family affair!"

The Chapel which had been built in Tudor times was lit by dozens of candles and the flowers brought hastily from the greenhouses scented the air with the fragrance of lilies and carnations.

There was no-one to give Marisa away, but the Duke took her up the short aisle on his arm and they were followed by Aline wearing her new dress.

With her red hair gleaming under the fragile veil, her eyes as brilliant as the diamond tiara, Marisa looked very lovely.

The Duke had been waiting for her in the Hall. As she came down the stairs, the train of her white gown rustling behind her, she knew he drew in his breath.

She reached his side. For a moment neither of them spoke, then he said in a low voice vibrant with emotion.

"I did not know that anyone could be so absolutely beautiful."

In the carved pews of the Chapel the members of the household sat in order of precedence. Miss Whitcham was in the place of honour, and after her came the whole staff down to the smallest boot boy who was squeezed in by the door and had no seat.

The service seemed to Marisa very moving.

There was a deep sincerity in the Duke's voice as he made his vows, and while she could hear the shyness in her own voice she prayed in her heart that she would never fail him.

She felt his fingers place the ring that had been his mother's on her finger. Then joining their hands together, the Chaplain pronounced them man and wife.

Marisa looked up into her husband's face and saw there so much love that for a moment she forgot everything in the joy of realising she was his.

From the Chapel the Duke led her to the big Banqueting Hall where despite such short notice the Chef had somehow concocted a cake which delighted Aline.

There was champagne for everyone in which to drink the health of the bride and bridegroom.

Turner made a speech wishing them every happiness and the Duke replied thanking them.

When the speeches were over, the Duke drew Marisa

away into the small Dining-Room where he usually dined
when he was alone or entertained only a few friends.

It was an oval room with magnificent pictures. The table was covered in white orchids and displayed all the
most famous gold candelabra and ornaments in the Milverley collection. Aline who had followed them said:

"Miss Whitcham says I'm to go to bed now."

"It is late," the Duke said, "and you must be tired."

"I am too excited to be tired," Aline replied, "but I will
go to bed because I expect you want to be alone."

"I have something exciting to tell you in the morning"
Marisa told her.

"But you are both going away," Aline said and her eyes
were suddenly wistful.

"That is what I am going to talk to you about," Marisa
said, "I have someone you will like very much. Her name
is Miss Meadfield and she is the person who first told me
all the stories I have told you."

"All the stories?" Aline asked, intrigued.

"Yes, and many many more I have not had time to tell
you as yet" Marisa said. "I want you to look after her and
get her to teach you the things she taught me while I was
a little girl. And while we are away your Papa has arranged with Miss Whitcham that there will be other children coming here every day to have lessons with you."

Marisa glanced up at the Duke mischievously as she
spoke and his eyes twinkled as he answered.

"You have taken the very words out of my mouth! Of
course that is exactly what I am telling Miss Whitcham to
do. You will like that."

"It sounds exciting" Aline replied, "but you will not
forget about me while you are away, will you?"

"I promise you we will never do that" Marisa answered, "and we will send you post-cards from every
place we stay so that you can see where we are. I know
Miss Meadfield will have lots of tales to tell you about the
towns and countries we visit."

"I shall be counting the days until you come back,"
Aline said.

"Well go to bed now," the Duke suggested, "or you will
be too tired to talk to us in the morning."

Aline lifted her face to his. He kissed her and then she put her arms round Marisa's neck.

"Goodnight . . . Mama" she whispered.

Then a little shy at the new word, she ran from the room.

"Let us have something to eat, my darling" the Duke suggested.

He drew Marisa to the table as Turner and the footmen came in carrying the first of many delicious dishes.

Later when the Housekeeper had helped Marisa undress and she was alone in the big State Bed-room, she sat down in front of the brightly burning fire on a white fur rug.

She had extinguished the candles, but the firelight made her hair which touched the ground around her glow red as the dancing flames.

The Duke came in to the room very quietly.

She did not rise, but lifted her face to his. He stood looking down at her, very tall in his brocade robe with its high collar and deep velvet cuffs.

"This is how I wanted to see you" he said in a deep voice. "If you only knew what I felt that night I came to the School-Room to find you holding that swine Freddy Farrington at pistol-point."

"I thought you were angry with me," Marisa answered.

"I was! Furiously angry!" the Duke replied, "and crazily jealous that another man should have seen your wonderful hair hanging over your shoulders."

"I had locked myself in my room, but Aline had a nightmare and I was forced to go to her."

"I thought it must be something like that," the Duke said. "You do not suppose that I would have imagined that you of all people would encourage someone like Farrington?"

"And yet he was your friend," Marisa questioned.

"One has friends and friends," the Duke said enigmatically. "I am not here, Marisa, to talk about friends, but about our love."

"I was thinking about you."

"And what were you thinking?"

He sat down as he spoke in the arm-chair looking at

her tiny straight nose etched against the darkness as her green eyes looked into the light of the fire.

"I was thinking that I love you" she said a little shyly. "I love you so much that I am afraid that I shall wake up and find this is all a dream—a wonderful dream that might so easily vanish."

"It will never vanish—that I promise you" the Duke answered. "You are mine, Marisa, as I meant you to be from the first moment I saw you. I have always known there was something missing in my life, and then when we met I knew it was you."

"How could you know that?" Marisa enquired.

"It was an instinct, so strong that it became an unarguable conviction" the Duke replied. "Do you believe, my precious, that we have been journeying towards each other ever since we were born?"

"I am sure of it" she answered, "and how terribly, terribly fortunate that we have found the person each of us was seeking."

She paused a moment then added:

"You told me, but I did not understand, that men and women seeking true love usually have to put up with what is false or imitation. Because we are so ... blessed, we must try to bring happiness to ... others."

"That is something you must teach me to do," the Duke said.

He rose to his feet as he spoke and reaching down drew Marisa into his arms, feeling the warmth of her body beneath her thin nightgown.

"I am so willing to learn" he said. "Are you, my darling, equally willing, to learn from me?"

"You know . . . I am" she whispered.

"I love you," he said, "I love you more than I can begin to tell you, and yet I know for both of us this is just the beginning. The beginning of a new life—a life that will be full and worthwhile. Oh, my little love, do not let me fail you."

His lips were on hers as he spoke and as he kissed her Marisa found herself drawing closer and closer to him until she felt a fire rising within her.

It was the fire which the Duke had called all-consuming

and which she knew now burnt away all that was false and ugly, leaving only what was true and beautiful.

This was the tidal wave that was irresistible and inescapable. This was an ecstasy so divine that made them not a man and woman, but one person at the feet of God.

"I . . . love . . . you" she murmured against his mouth.

The Duke raised his head and looked down at her parted lips, her eyelids heavy with the passion he had awakened in her and her red hair streaming over his arm.

"I worship you my precious," he said hoarsely.

He was kissing her again. His lips lingered on her mouth then sought the softness of her white neck.

"Does that make you feel excited?" he asked.

"Y-yes" she whispered.

"And wild?"

"Yes . . . yes."

"Oh my darling! My little love—my wife!"

The Duke lifted her in his arms and Marisa could only surrender to him, her body, heart and soul as he carried her into the shadows.

ABOUT THE AUTHOR

BARBARA CARTLAND, the celebrated romantic author, historian, playwright, lecturer, political speaker and television personality, has now written 135 books. Mrs. Cartland has had a number of historical books published and several biographical ones, including that of her brother, Major Ronald Cartland, who was the first Member of Parliament to be killed in the War. This book had a preface by Sir Winston Churchill.

In private life, Barbara Cartland, who is a Commander of the Order of St. John of Jerusalem, has fought for better conditions and salaries for Midwives and Nurses. As President of the Royal College of Midwives (Hertfordshire Branch), she has been invested with the first Badge of Office ever given in Great Britain, which was subscribed to by the Midwives themselves. She has also championed the cause for old people and founded the first Romany Gypsy Camp in the world.

Mrs. Cartland is deeply interested in Vitamin Therapy and is President of the British National Association for Health.

Barbara Cartland

The world's bestselling author of romantic fiction. Her stories are always captivating tales of intrigue, adventure and love.

☐	LESSONS IN LOVE	8261	95¢
☐	THE DARING DECEPTION	8265	95¢
☐	NO DARKNESS FOR LOVE	8275	95¢
☐	THE LITTLE ADVENTURE	8278	95¢

Ask for them at your local bookseller or use this handy coupon:

Bantam Books, Inc., Dept. BC, 414 East Golf Road, Des Plaines, Ill. 60016

Please send me the books I have checked above. I am enclosing $_____ (please add 25¢ to cover postage and handling). Send check or money order—no cash or C.O.D.'s please.

Mr/Mrs/Miss_____

Address_____

City_____ State/Zip_____

BC—3/74

Please allow three weeks for delivery. This offer expires 3/75.